FOUR STORIES BY INGMAR BERGMAN

Four Screenplays of Ingmar Bergman

Scenes from a Marriage

Three Films by Ingmar Bergman:
Through a Glass Darkly,
Winter Light,
and *The Silence*

Bergman: Persona and Shame

The Seventh Seal

Wild Strawberries

Face to Face

FOUR STORIES BY
INGMAR BERGMAN

The Touch
Cries and Whispers
The Hour of the Wolf
The Passion of Anna

Translated from the Swedish by Alan Blair

SONOMA CO. LIBRARY

Anchor Press/Doubleday, Garden City, New York
1976

ISBN: 0-385-00778-7
LIBRARY OF CONGRESS CATALOG CARD NUMBER 76-2754
ANCHOR PRESS EDITION: 1976
COPYRIGHT © 1976 BY DOUBLEDAY & COMPANY, INC.
ALL RIGHTS RESERVED
PRINTED IN THE UNITED STATES OF AMERICA
FIRST EDITION

CONTENTS

THE TOUCH

It is hard to write a screenplay, but I wonder whether it isn't just as hard to read it. The words can never express what the finished film wants to convey. Sometimes there are too many, piling up in a jumble on top of the spontaneous feeling. Sometimes there are too few, leaving the reader in the lurch in the most shameful way. In any case, a filmscript is always a half-finished product, a pale and uncertain reflection.

This is particularly true of a film like *The Touch*. If, with any pretensions to completeness, I were to reproduce in words what happens in the film I have conceived, I would be forced to write a bulky book of little readable value and great nuisance. I have neither the talent nor the patience for heroic exercises of that kind. Besides, such a procedure would effectively kill all creative joy for both me and the artists. I therefore offer the reader a rather summary text, a cipher, which at best appeals to his imagination and insight.

Regarding the completed film I can be brief for now: Its colors are warm. The keys in which it is set are fairly bright—intimacy, tenderness, and a touch of melancholy. Further explanations would be absurd. Films resemble people. You like them, you don't like them, or you're indifferent to them. In this particular case it is my will, my hope, my wish that you may like it.

INGMAR BERGMAN

1.

The old red-brick façade of the hospital stands behind the autumn trees. The ward is on the second floor. In a small recreation room on a landing a very old woman dressed in a lay sister's uniform can be glimpsed. She is standing by the window, letting the sun shine into her eyes; her hands are clasped beneath her breast. Karin stops for a moment; the old woman takes no notice of her.

In the long, dark corridor of the ward, with doors on either side, the ceiling lights are already on—it is an autumn afternoon. Nurses hurry from room to room with the dinner trays.

Karin at once catches sight of the doctor, who comes toward her with his hand extended: "Your mother died about a quarter of an hour ago, without any real struggle; it was all very peaceful."

Karin asks if she may go into the sickroom and the sister opens the outer door for her, letting it close silently behind her. The inner door is ajar and Karin can see the end of the bed, and the big dark tree outside the window. She goes in slowly.

When she sees the dead woman her eyes fill with tears and she whispers: "Poor, poor, poor darling . . ." The dead woman is lying with her head turned to the side; her eyes are closed, her mouth is slightly open, and her teeth are just visible behind her yellow lips. Her thick gray hair is combed back from her low broad forehead, which has been furrowed by pain. But her face bears no trace of suffering. Rather, there is a mysterious smile: the deep wrinkles of laughter at the eyes, the soft, upturned corners of the mouth. Her hands are resting on the quilt—short, broad hands with square fingertips and short nails. There is a small bandage on one forefinger.

Karin sits down in the visitor's chair. The window is ajar and the murmur of distant traffic can be heard. Time and again she passes her hand over her eyes, time and again she chokes back a sob. All is still, except for the little clock ticking busily on the bedside table.

At last Karin moves close to the bed, bends over her mother's face, and kisses her on the cheek. She stands for quite a long time looking at her; she imagines that the eyelids quiver, that the breast rises and falls with breathing, but it is an optical illusion—death's enigmatic game with the senses of the living.

The ward sister comes up to her in the corridor. Karin thanks her for all the help and care. The sister asks what she would like done with the personal effects. Karin says they will be fetched tomorrow. "What about the wedding rings, would you like those now?" Before Karin has time to reply the sister has gone to get them. "Here they are." Now they are lying in Karin's open hand. Two thick gold rings worn for fifty years. Inside one of them is engraved "Henrik" and the date, inside the other only "Henrik." They are the worse for wear and badly scratched.

Karin thanks the woman, no longer aware of what she is saying. The cloakroom, in a corner just outside the glass doors of the ward, is dark. Now Karin is standing there with her face turned to the protective darkness, weeping to herself at the unutterable sense of loss.

Someone stops and turns back. He stands for a moment rather discreetly a few paces away, then finally asks in English: "Can I do something for you?"

Karin turns her tear-stained face toward the visitor: "Please leave me alone," she says, also in English. The man looks taken aback and very embarrassed. He mumbles an apology. Karin turns away and blows her nose. When she looks up again he has gone. A moment or two later her brothers and sisters and other relations begin to arrive.

2.

"The garden is our pride and joy," Karin says in her best English to David.

"We're both very fond of flowers, trees, and shrubs," Andreas adds, putting his arm around his wife's shoulders.

They are strolling around together in the autumn splendor; it is a mild Sunday afternoon with the scent of summer still lingering in the air.

"We work in the garden every spare minute. You must come here one spring or early summer. It's so beautiful then, you can't imagine. In the wintertime we picture what we're going to plant and alter. Our daughter likes gardening too. She has a corner of her own over there that she looks after herself."

Inside the house the telephone rings and the daughter, Agnes, who is fourteen, calls: "Daddy's wanted on the phone."

Andreas excuses himself and leaves Karin with the guest.

At first they are silent, then Karin asks with a smile if David really is interested in gardening and in flowers and trees. He grins and says he couldn't care less about them. They both laugh. "I must go and see to the joint," Karin says. "Will you excuse me a minute?" She disappears toward the back of the house.

David looks about him. The house is spacious and rather old-fashioned, not very beautiful. The garden surrounds it, and there's a huge maple on either side. Shouts and laughter can be heard from the lawn next door; two young girls are playing badminton somewhat half-heartedly. An upstairs window is thrown open and a ten-year-old boy hangs out perilously by one arm and launches a model airplane, which sways in the breeze. "Hallo," David calls in

Swedish. "Hallo," the boy says. The plane lands in a tree and he vanishes from the window.

Karin is back. "Agnes is awfully capable," she says in her circumspect and rather careful English. "Actually she's doing the cooking, and she gets angry with me if I go in and supervise. She thinks you're interesting," she adds with a laugh. "She thinks you look like a film star. Anders, don't forget to have a bath and change your shirt before dinner," she says abruptly to her son, who is just scrambling down from the tree with his airplane.

"Oh, don't keep nagging me," Anders replies.

"I can see why you like it here, you and Andreas," David says politely, making conversation.

"This house was left to Andreas by his parents," Karin says. "We'd never dream of living right in town or near the hospital. Andreas needs this relaxation, he works far too hard."

"The marriage is a happy one?" David asks, with only faint irony. Karin glances at him and smiles.

"The marriage is most unusually happy," she says. "We've been married for sixteen years."

"So everything in the garden's lovely," David says with a laugh. Karin stops and grows serious, thinking hard.

"It's awfully difficult talking about this sort of thing," she says after a while. "Especially when you have to speak a foreign language."

"I don't want to be tactless," David says. Karin looks at him in surprise. Suddenly he gives in. "Forgive me," he says quietly.

The conversation flags, but it doesn't really matter. "Would you like a drink?" Karin asks suddenly.

"I was wondering when you were going to ask," David replies. They both laugh.

Andreas is standing on the steps. "A drink?" he says. "We'll have it outside, eh? I'm just coming. Whiskey, is that right?" They sit down in the swing sofa. Andreas can be seen in the living room, busy with the drinks.

"I keep thinking of our first meeting," David says unexpectedly.

"At the hospital?"

"Yes, when you stood crying in the cloakroom. I suppose it's hardly the thing to tell you, but I fell in love with you. I didn't mean you ever to know. But as chance or whatever it is has made us friends, I can't help telling you. I'm in love with you, Karin. I don't want to worry you or upset you with this confession. But I'm in love with you, and I want you to know it."

"No, thanks," David says. "The dinner was delicious, but I really couldn't eat any more. I must say Agnes is a superb cook. Yes, they stumbled on her while restoring a church a few miles from here, near the dig where I'm working. The old medieval church of Hammar, if you know it. Well, they were making a hole in the wall. When they'd got about halfway through they found a cavity. They started taking the wall down, very, very carefully. Yes, please, I'd like some coffee. What was I saying now? Oh yes, presently they began to see something dimly in there in the darkness. It was a woman's face—a well-preserved wooden sculpture representing the Holy Virgin. No, they haven't got her out yet. It takes a very long time. You have to go terribly slowly so as not to damage anything—there might be other objects inside the cavity. As far as we know, this sculpture is something very rare. But the strangest thing of all is how did it come to your country? How did it end up in this remote medieval church? And last, but most important: why did they wall it up! Oh, thank you, a whiskey please . . . No thanks, no ice. So far all we can see is a glimpse of her face and the top of the body behind the stone wall."

Andreas has photographed a lot of his flowers. Later that evening he is showing his pictures and commenting on them. David listens with a polite smile, assuring him that there's nothing he likes better than watching amateur films. Interspersed among trees and flowers are shots of the children, of Karin. For a few short moments the mother is glimpsed—always summer, sea, and sunlight. Now and then Karin says this can't possibly interest David. Andreas says, "Just at the end of this reel I'm sure there are some fantastic shots of an orchid I found quite by chance. Yes, there it is, look at it, just look. Look at the color. Look at it."

Karin glances at David to see if he is watching. He is sitting with his face turned to the screen but with a faraway look in his eyes. He has been drinking rather heavily during the evening and there are beads of perspiration on his forehead. His figure is slumped and he has an air of weariness and boredom. Suddenly he turns his face to Karin and looks at her. She meets his eyes and gives a little conventional smile.

"Haven't you any pictures of your wife in the nude?" David asks suddenly. "I'd like to see what Karin looks like in the nude."

Andreas gives a good-humored laugh and replies that David will have to content himself with the orchids.

The guest makes a move fairly early. Andreas offers to drive him home, but he declines with a laugh and tells them not to worry, there won't be any scandal. He embraces Andreas heartily and they pat each other on the back. Then he embraces Karin, gives her a clumsy kiss, and departs. Andreas and Karin go around the house turning out lights and locking up. They let the dog out, then go in to Agnes, who is reading in bed. Anders is already asleep in his little room beyond the kitchen. "Good night, Agnes, thanks so much for all your help."

"I didn't think much of that David," Agnes says.

"Didn't you?" Karin says in surprise.

"No, I didn't like him," Agnes maintains.

"Why not?" Karin asks, hunting for something in Agnes's drawer. "Where's that bra I was going to exchange for you?"

"In the other drawer, Mommy," Agnes says irritably. Karin finds what she is looking for and wishes her daughter good night once more. What was wrong with David she never found out.

Husband and wife get ready for bed in the bedroom they share. They pass in and out of the bathroom, chatting quietly. "What time must you be at the hospital tomorrow?"

"Seven o'clock, I've an operation at half-past."

"What did you think of David?"

"I think he's a damned nice chap."

"Didn't he drink rather a lot?"

"Did he? It never struck me." Andreas sounds genuinely astonished. "Well, you know, foreigners!"

"How did you and David come to meet?" Karin asks suddenly. Andreas hesitates a moment.

"He had an attack of kidney stones and Jacobi at the Museum rang and asked me to look after him. That's how it was."

They get into bed at almost the same time. Andreas says, "Blast, I had planned to make love to you, but now I'm so damned sleepy."

Karin laughs and says she too is awfully tired. "I'm not even up to reading tonight," Andreas says, with a huge yawn.

"Nor am I," Karin says, catching the yawn.

"Let's go to sleep then," Andreas says, putting out the light. "Where's your hand?"

"Here's my hand!"

"It's good to hold your hand."

Silence, they doze. "Have you taken the pill?" Andreas murmurs.

"It won't matter if I miss it tonight, will it?"

"Matter," Andreas says with a slight laugh.

3.

It is a still, cloudy autumn day. The plain little church lies on a rise above the surrounding countryside. Nearby stands an ancient stone tower. There is scaffolding here and there, but it is Saturday and no workmen are to be seen. Inside the bare church the warmth of summer lingers; there is the smell of rotten wood and gentle decay. To the left of the altar, beside the entrance to the vestry, is the breach in the wall. Higher up runs a frieze of medieval, half-obliterated paintings representing the life and passion of Christ from the annunciation to the crucifixion. The reredos is a peasant depiction of the Last Supper.

"Karin, come and have a look," David says. He has removed a piece of sacking, which partially conceals the hole in the wall. "Stand on that box and lean inward." He switches on a flashlight and directs it into the mysterious dark cavity. "Can you see her?" Dimly illuminated by the daylight and David's flashlight, the madonna turns her face to Karin and gazes at her with a faint smile. She is an earthly woman, no halo. The contours of the body are round and sensual, the hands holding the naked, refractory child are broad working hands. Her thighs and breasts swell beneath the ingeniously carved medieval raiment; she sits leaning slightly forward as if to stop the child from climbing down out of her lap. But her eyes are turned on the beholder, as though on a visitor who enters unexpectedly, and the smile is trusting, with no anxiety.

Outside, by the church wall, the air is mild, like summer. David and Karin sit down on a wide plank and have a view over the countryside and the sea. They are surrounded by complete stillness.

"Give me your hand," David says. She hesitates, takes off her glove and puts out her hand to him. He holds it between his two hands, raises it to his cheek, then kisses the palm. She pulls her hand back quickly and gets up.

"No," she says, "no, not that! Just what do you want of me?" He doesn't answer at first.

"I don't know," he says at last. "I want you."

"Why?" she asks.

"I'm in love with you. Isn't that enough?"

She shakes her head. "I've been married for sixteen years. I've never been unfaithful to Andreas. Not once. I don't want to start lying and sneaking and living a peculiar double life. Perhaps you think I'm silly, but I'm not sure it's worth such a big sacrifice. Do you see what I mean? It's hard to explain this in a foreign language. Forgive me. I can't explain anything."

He bends forward to kiss her, but she evades him. "No," she says, "no. If you kiss me, then . . . then I don't know. I don't know." She is still smiling, but is very upset. Then she says suddenly, very soberly, that she must hurry home.

They stop just outside the garden gate and he asks when he can see her again. She answers promptly: "Tomorrow's Sunday and I can't, and on Monday we're having a big turn-out, two charwomen are coming to do the autumn cleaning and I can't possibly get away, but on Tuesday we can meet."

"Where?" David asks impatiently.

"I'll come to your place at half-past two," she replies in a matter-of-fact tone. Then she kisses him lightly on the cheek and takes refuge behind the garden gate.

In the hall, she takes off her coat and hangs it up, then looks at herself in the mirror, examining her face. She hears Andreas speaking on the phone in his study, goes in to him at once, and sits down in his swivel chair. He's standing at the desk talking to a colleague: "She'd better go in straightaway, I'll ring the hospital and fix a bed for her. I'll see you tomorrow, we can have lunch together, you come up to my room, will you? I'll be there from twelve-thirty onward." She swivels on the chair and looks at her husband with interest. He smiles at her and purses his lips in a comic way. Then he puts the phone down. "Did you enjoy your drive?"

"It was awfully interesting," Karin replies.

"Why didn't you ask David to dinner?"

"I did, but he wouldn't come."

Andreas calls the hospital: "Good afternoon, this is the head, may I speak to Sister Gunhild in ward 3. Thank you. I'll wait."

Karin gets up and goes toward the door. "I'll go down and relieve Agnes in the kitchen, she's going out with some friends this evening."

"She must be home by two at the latest," her father decrees.

"We can talk about it later," Karin says evasively.

"Oh, I see, well, will you please ask Sister Gunhild to call me the minute she's free. Thank you."

"Uh, there's something I'd like to tell you," Karin says at the door.

"Sounds exciting," Andreas says. His eyes blink behind his thick glasses and he is smiling in surprise.

But Karin changes her mind, and says instead: "I don't think I want any help in the house after all. It's much better to manage everything yourself, you avoid such a lot of vexation."

"Is *that* what you wanted to tell me?" Andreas asks.

"Yes . . . why?"

"You started off so seriously, I thought it was something important."

4.

She is very nervous but quite gay; she has entrenched herself in a sturdy pair of slacks and a large jumper. Her hair is properly combed and she has spectacles on her nose. "I must wear specs when I drive a car," she explains. She takes off her coat and looks around at the dreary, temporarily rented apartment. "I had an awful trouble finding it. This old part of the town has one-way streets going the wrong way coming from us. I thought I'd never find it. Sorry I'm late."

David has bought sherry and laid glasses ready. He has also bought some flowers, which are already wilting. "Poor flowers," Karin says. "I'll slit their stalks and perhaps they'll revive." She is busy with this in the kitchenette. "How did you come by this apartment?"

"A colleague," David says, trying to speak distinctly.

"It's a horribly dreary place, don't you think?"

"I hadn't thought of it," David replies apologetically. "It's better than staying at a hotel anyway."

"Yes, it's better *now*," Karin says, smiling at him.

The flowers are on the table. "Would you like some sherry?" David asks.

"What I'd like is a cup of tea," Karin says, peeping into the kitchen cupboard. "Have you any tea?"

"I'm afraid I'm out of it. I'll run out and get some if you like."

"No, no, let's have your sherry."

He gets the bottle open after a certain amount of difficulty; when he begins to pour the sherry his hand is shaking so violently that he spills it on the table. "Are you nervous, David?" Karin asks, with a smile.

"Yes, my pulse is 690," he replies. "Aren't *you* nervous?"

"I'm almost fainting," Karin says with a laugh. They toast each other in silence. "Excuse this ugly jumper and these old slacks. I wanted to be wearing a pretty dress when I came to you for the first time, but it suddenly turned awfully cold."

David smiles politely and says he even thought he saw some flakes of snow in all the rain. "I hate it when it's cold," Karin says, frowning. "It's a wretched climate here on the coast. The spring's always late."

"Yes, but it has been an unusually nice autumn," David says, pouring out more sherry.

"Not for me, thanks," Karin says, holding up her hand. "It has already gone to my head. What shall we talk about now?" They both laugh. "What shall we do now?"

"Let's get undressed and get into bed and see what happens," Karin says. "But we'll draw the curtains, eh? I'm rather shy."

"So am I," David says.

When David comes back from the bathroom, wearing his threadbare old dressing gown, Karin is standing naked in the dusk of the room, looking at herself in a solid old mirror that, for no particular reason, is hanging in one corner. She turns to him with a quick smile, and as he goes to put his arms around her she pushes him carefully away. "Wait," she says, "wait a bit. You must look at me first." He sits down on the bed and she stands in front of him.

"I am thirty-four," she says with a smile. "You can see that from my face, especially around the eyes. I have borne two children, whom I have suckled. My breasts were nicer before. And I've a wrinkle here on my belly from my second child; Anders was so big, you see. I'm not a very experienced mistress. Andreas and I have always had it good together in bed. There have never been any problems, even if it hasn't always been so passionate. My legs are on the short side and my bottom's a bit too big—it used to worry me a lot when I was a girl. I don't want you to act in any special way in order to satisfy me, if you know what I mean. It will only make me anxious and tense. I've no idea why I've come here to you today or why I'm going to bed with you. I don't even know if I'm in love with you.

I've just fallen for you, I suppose, and it excites me very much when you say you're in love with me and you want me.

"Forgive me for talking so much. I suppose it's not a very good way of beginning an affair, but I've never been in this situation. I've only had two men before you and the first one I don't even remember, so Andreas is really the only one that counts. Of course I've terrible pangs of conscience for being unfaithful to him now. But he need never know anything. I'm never going to leave him. He's the best person in the world for me. David, my dear, forgive me for saying all this, but I want you to know who you're going to bed with. Perhaps it doesn't mean anything much to you, and maybe I'm making a lot of fuss about this little affair, but for me it isn't a little affair. Now let's get into bed and you can warm me, because I feel awfully cold."

David has listened smilingly to this long speech and as she gets into bed beside him he puts his arms around her and kisses her gently on the lips. Then they lie still, looking at each other.

"You've even put clean sheets on for us," Karin says. She is thoughtful for a while. "Have you had other women here in this bed? No, you needn't answer, it was a silly question. Put your hand on my breast." They kiss again.

"It's no good, I can't today," David says suddenly.

"Did my long speech frighten you?" Karin asks, with a smile. "It doesn't matter. As long as we're here with one another. It's good as it is."

About an hour later she says softly: "I must go now, David. I promised to meet Andreas at the airport. He has been to Stockholm today." They look at each other and kiss, then Karin gets up and begins to dress quickly.

"Come here," he says suddenly, sitting up in bed with two pillows behind his back. She goes over to him and he takes her hand. "I want to tell you something," David says slowly. "But I don't know how to put it." His face is pale and the eyes are red-rimmed. "I don't know how to say it."

Sitting down on the bed, she puts her arms around his shoulders and draws him to her, slowly stroking his ear and cheek. "I'm so fond of you," she says in her own language. "I'm so very very fond of you."

Then she gets up gently and finishes dressing. He gets out of bed and puts on an old dressing gown. As she is about to go she gives him a quick kiss.

"Are you disappointed in me?" David asks.

She hugs him and starts to laugh. She laughs and coaxes him to laugh. She holds her arms around him and says, with a smile: "No no no no no no no!" Then she hurries out, but discovers at once that she has forgotten her gloves and knocks on the door. He opens it. "I forgot my gloves," she says, rather rushed but still smiling. He grabs at her and kisses her passionately. She feels his desire and is about to give in to a sudden impulse, but says: "I can't now, not now. I'll come back another day. Soon. I'll phone you tomorrow morning."

5.

"Hallo, it's Karin. Have you been waiting? I didn't want to ring until I was alone in the house. I was so worried you'd already left."

"I didn't think I'd hear from you. I don't know why. Incidentally, I'm not quite sober. I took a sleeping pill but couldn't get to sleep. So then I had a drink and took another pill. I should have been out at the dig at eight-fifteen or eight-thirty at the latest. But I'm not going today. I've a right to be sick sometimes too. You mustn't mind my being a bit stoned, I'm not in the habit of it. I didn't think you'd ring. I didn't think we'd meet again. I'm . . . I'd like to explain something to you. It's funny, there's something important I'd like to tell you, something I've never told a living soul. I'd like to tell you, but I've no words. I'm mentally illiterate. Can't you come to me now, this instant? I'm longing for you. What are you doing? Are you going to make the beds and tidy up, or what are you going to do? Are you going out to do the shopping for dinner? Are you a blasted domestic service agency or what the hell are you? Can't you come at once? Can't you come?"

"I can't come now. I can't, you must understand. I can't just drop everything. David, are you there? Why don't you answer?"

"I see," David says distantly. Then there is silence.

"I'll come then. But I haven't time to stay more than a little while."

6.

So she does go after all, very upset and without really wanting to. When they meet she is anxious and cold. The room has not been aired and stinks of stale cigarette smoke. He is unshaven and only half dressed, and reeks of liquor and nocturnal terrors. He throws his arms around her and pulls her coat off. She resists feebly, saying she has no time to stay. He mumbles something she doesn't catch; it sounds like a word of abuse. There is a short struggle beside the unmade bed, he forces her down and starts tearing her clothes off. Pale with rage and humiliation, Karin tells him to stop it, she'll undress herself. She pulls off her pantyhose and briefs, drags her skirt up, lies down on the bed, and opens her legs. He climbs on top of her and thrusts into her without kissing her or embracing her. She keeps her eyes shut tight and lets him get on with it. He moans faintly and frantically; he is tense and unfeeling. She opens her eyes and looks at him. His face is sallow with hatred, and black rings have sunk in deep under his eyes. "Don't look at me, for Christ's sake," he mutters in a thick voice, laying his right hand over her face. Then he says some words in a foreign language. It sounds frightening. His mouth opens and the lips are drawn aside, baring the teeth; his body contracts violently and out of his throat comes a sound which is either a sob or a smothered scream of pain. Then they lie silent and remote, their clothes and the bedclothes in a heap, their bodies heavy with disgust and loneliness. The morning light is harsh and gray outside the big window with its torn curtains. Karin frees herself, gets up, and goes into the bathroom.

7.

That afternoon Andreas and Karin work in the garden, gathering all the windfalls into big baskets. It is drizzling but not particularly cold. The sun is sulking behind the rainclouds but breaks through now and then in burning rays under the aged trees.

"I rang you several times this morning," Andreas says in passing, "but there was no answer."

"No, I was in the attic, tidying up. We've lots of old clothes hanging up there which I've started sorting out to send to the Red Cross."

"Good idea," Andreas says, straightening his back. "Are you worried about something?"

Karin doesn't answer at once. "It's nothing," she says. "My period's coming on and that always makes me a bit melancholy."

"Nothing else?" Andreas asks gently.

"No, I don't think so," Karin replies, with a smile. Then she goes up to her husband and puts her arm around him.

8.

Just below the old church they have found the remains of a monastery and a grave-field from the second century b.c.; the remains are very sparse and difficult to define. The area has been roped off and is partly uncovered. From the church a drill can be heard, and the blows of picks. Outside it is quiet. Two men dressed in thick overalls are lying flat on their faces poking at the earth with small metal spades. It is an autumn day, restless, with abrupt changes between light and rain shadows. Karin approaches shyly and stops some distance away, not daring to go up. David catches sight of her, says something to his fellow worker, brushes the soil off his knees, and comes up to her. His face is grave, almost off-putting.

"Why haven't you got in touch?" Karin asks at once. "I've tried several times to ring you, but there's no answer, and yesterday I went and rang your doorbell and I could hear you were at home but you didn't open the door."

David has taken her by the arm and is leading her through the field and over toward the edge of the woods. They sit down behind some trees that still have their leaves, beside a quiet pool of water.

"Why do you go on like this?" she asks. "I can't bear your silence, it's the only thing I can't bear." Suddenly she caresses his face.

"It's nothing," he says. "If only you'll have patience with me."

"I've all the patience in the world," Karin says, with a smile. "I've no demands. Don't think I'm making any demands. I don't understand myself what has happened. All I know is that I can't think one thought that you are not mixed up in. I can't live one minute without your being part of that very minute. That's how it is."

David nods. "I don't know what to do with all these churned-up feelings."

Karin fondles his face again. "As long as we don't lose each other it doesn't matter," she says quickly and softly. "That's what is so important. That you don't leave me outside. I'd be utterly powerless then."

There's nothing much more they can say. They sit looking at each other, caressing each other with awkward, clumsy gestures.

"I wish I could explain to you," David says.

"I know," Karin says. "I know."

He strokes her and she gets dirt on her cheek.

9.

A poem by Gunnar Ekelöf

Wake me to sleep in you
wake my worlds to you
light my dead stars nearer you.

Dream me away out of my world
home to the home of the flames
give birth to me, live me, kill me nearer you.

Nearer me to you
nearer the hearth of birth
take me warmer, take me nearer you.

10.

It is winter. They meet for a few hours almost every afternoon, always in his shabby, rented apartment. One day while she is helping him tidy up she finds an album full of old photographs on the bookshelf. She sits down by the window looking through it. He bends over her.

"I cart that photo album around with me wherever I go," David says. "I don't know why. Presumably a sort of obscure sentimentality. My father and mother, all my relatives are dead. We lived in Berlin, just outside the city. My father was head of a private mental clinic. I was fourteen when Father suddenly sent Mother and me and my sister to Switzerland. Six months later we lost touch with our relatives in Germany. They were wiped out in various camps. After the war and Mother's death I went to Israel, where I was trained. I think I keep that album for Mother's sake. Here she is as a girl, just engaged. Don't you think she's pretty? She was warm and impulsive, passionate and quick-tempered. She was inclined to be strict, except when we were ill. Then there was no limit to her tenderness. Sometimes it feels so utterly lonely without Mother, isn't it absurd? After all, I'm grown up. I remember when she was expecting my sister. I couldn't have been more than six. One morning by mistake I saw Mother naked, with her great belly. I was scared and started to cry. Mother put her arms around me; I remember I only had a singlet on and felt cold. Mother took me into bed with her. She was still naked and I was allowed to feel her tummy and I could feel with my hand how the baby kept moving. I remember it very vividly, but Mother denied it all when I reminded her about it after I grew up. She was even rather annoyed."

"You had a sister?" Karin asks.

"Yes, here she is, we were inseparable as children, we always played together, although I was six years older."

"Where's your sister now?" Karin asks.

David sits silent for a moment. "She's gone," he says. "I've no family, no relations. I've been married, but it was a disaster for us both."

"Did your sister die during the war?" Karin persists.

"I don't know," David replies irritably. "She's gone. I know nothing about her."

11.

David is furious but controls himself. He smiles as he opens the door to Karin. It is late afternoon. "Where have you been? I've been waiting for you."

"You can't have been, I said I'd be late today."

"You said you'd be here at three o'clock, and now it's four."

"I remember particularly I never said a time, as I knew I couldn't be punctual—I didn't know how long the lunch was going to last."

Karin smiles and kisses him on the lips, and takes off her fur coat. She is dressed in her finery today, with jewelry and high-heeled shoes. "So I didn't say a time," she says, kissing him again. "But as you were so persistent I promised to come anyway, even if it could only be for a short while. How dark it is in here, shall we put the light on?" Karin is in a very good mood. Exhilarated, amused by David's anger.

He takes her by the arms and kisses her roughly. "You've been smoking," he exclaims crossly.

"Yes, I have," she says, with a smile.

"But we'd promised each other to give it up."

"Yes, but today I couldn't resist it after all that good food. I've smoked five cigarettes," she says, holding up five fingers and laughing. "Oh, aren't you cross now!"

"Not in the least," he says icily, "but we had an agreement. And you've been drinking a lot, too."

"Yes, I have," Karin says, nodding many times. "I think I'm a bit tipsy. I'm a little tipsy. I really am squiffy. Come and take me now. I'm in rather a hurry. At least give me a kiss and say you forgive me."

She embraces him and kisses him. He strikes her across the face. She stumbles to one side; the blow has caught her hard on the cheek and mouth. Tears of rage, amazement, and humiliation spring to her eyes. David seizes a chair and hurls it along the floor; it ends up broken in a corner.

"No one has ever struck me," Karin says after a while. "I've never been hit in all my life."

"I hate it when you're like that," David snarls, livid with rage.

"I was merely gay."

"You're not sober, and you've been smoking," he shouts, beside himself.

"*I was gay,*" Karin repeats. "I've been to a lunch for a foreign delegation, I told you beforehand. I've enjoyed myself. Andreas *wondered very much* why I was in such a hurry. It was difficult for me to come here today. But I came because you kept on at me."

"I can't stand that goddamn Andreas," David shouts. "That blasted hypocritical idiot and bungler. He can go to hell!"

"You're crazy. Stop shouting like that." Karin begins to laugh. "Heavens, you do look angry!"

"Get out," he says coldly. "Go to hell. Go home to your blasted paragon. That's the place for you. There's no point in our going on like this. Do you hear what I say? Go to hell and leave me in peace."

"Now you're being silly," Karin says calmly, putting on her fur coat.

But his impotent rage isn't spent yet. "I'm tired of you, I'm glad it's all over. I'm bored and fed up, do you hear?"

Karin stops, turns around, looks at him. "Poor David," she says in a different tone of voice. "Poor David and poor Karin. What a hard time we're going to have."

"That's why it's much better to break it off now, this instant," David answers mockingly.

Karin shakes her head, she is sad now. "If only it were so simple," she says. Then she goes to him and looks at him gravely, searchingly. "If you want me for anything you can ring me as usual tomorrow morning." She strokes his cheek quickly.

When she gets outside the door, she stops for a moment to listen. It is quite silent. She walks slowly downstairs, and now she begins to weep. It is not even proper weeping, it is more like an unbearable weight, a sudden insight. She goes down step by step, holding on to the rail. As she is about to go out into the steet she bumps into a woman who nods to her and gives her an inquisitive smile. She nods back and opens the street door. Then she hears him, bounding down the stairs after her.

They are back in the darkening room. They are back in each other, in tenderness and intimacy and forgiveness, but also in a secret despair which aches deep down in their innermost communion.

12.

That evening Andreas and Karin are sitting, each in a comfortable chair, in his study playing chess. The phonograph is playing softly. The dog is asleep on the rug. Anders comes in with a Coca-Cola and sinks into an armchair.

"Was it a good film?" Andreas asks.

"Not very," the boy replies. "A lot of silly love-making, it's so boring."

"Oh, wasn't there any other film?" Karin asks.

"No, I've seen the others."

"Are you hungry?" Karin asks again.

"No, I just made myself a sandwich."

"Good night."

"Who's winning?"

"Mommy always does," Andreas replies.

"Good night."

Anders heaves himself out of the chair and disappears. "I'll come up and say good night and put the light out in a little while," Karin calls, but Anders makes no answer to this.

"Where's Agnes?" her father asks.

"She's at a dance, you know that."

"But she had such a bad cold."

"Not this evening. Agnes is never ill on a Saturday."

Andreas glances up and gives a quick smile. "What's that sore on your lip?"

"I don't know what it can be," Karin says with a shrug. "I only saw it myself a while ago. Can it be lack of vitamins?"

"I hardly think so," Andreas says, with a smile.

They go on playing for a while in silence. "I have to attend a congress in Rome in April, would you like to come with me?" he asks.

"That sounds awfully nice," Karin says evasively. "Rome's lovely in April, isn't it? I'm not sure that I can. I'll have to get someone to come and look after the children."

"That's already fixed," Andreas says gaily. "I rang my sister Eva this afternoon and she said it suited her very well. She liked the sound of it very much. She's so lonely now after her divorce, poor thing."

"Let's think about it," Karin says.

"Well, you don't seem very enthusiastic," Andreas says, rather crestfallen.

"Oh, you know what I'm like," Karin replies, with an apologetic smile. "Forgive me."

Andreas stretches and yawns. "Yes, I know what you're like. Let's go to bed. You'll win this game anyway. I'll just let Fia out." He calls the dog. Karin puts the glasses on a tray, turns off the phonograph, and puts out the light.

They get undressed. Andreas is standing in front of the big mirror in the dressing room, naked. He calls to Karin. She's already in her nightie and has a hairbrush in her hand. He stands her in front of him and pulls off her nightie. He gazes closely at her for a long time in the mirror. She endures this with sudden submissiveness. Turning her toward him, he kisses her on the mouth beside the sore. Then, laying her down on the rug, he makes love to her, slowly and with all his conjugal experience.

13.

It is a sunny, windy day in early spring. The Holy Virgin has been lifted out of her cavity and put back in her exalted position in the gently restored church, which smells of fresh paint and new timber. The grave-field on the slope has been explored, excavated, photographed, and registered. Up in the organ loft a small choir is rehearsing for Sunday's reconsecration.

"The madonna wasn't quite such a treasure as we first thought," David says. "But she'll do. They think she came here from Denmark in the thirteenth century."

"Why was she walled up?" Karin asks.

"Nobody knows. Maybe she was too worldly."

"I'm going to come and see her sometimes," Karin says. "Once you've gone and I'm left alone."

"Are you a believer?" David asks.

"No," Karin replies. "I'm not a believer."

They sit down by the wall of the church; the sunshine is bright and warm. They sit close together, listening to the singing. "When do you leave?" Karin asks.

"Tomorrow, early."

"When will you be back?"

"In about six months—September or October."

"How long will you stay then?"

"About the same length of time."

"What are you going to do when you get back to London?"

"I shall prepare a series of lectures. Eighteen of them."

"In the summer?"

"Yes, in the summer."

They sit in silence. The music is louder now. "Will you write to me?" Karin asks.

"I'll write whenever I have a spare moment."

"You'll get letters from me too." Once again, there is silence and the melancholy of parting.

"We've lived together for six months," Karin says quietly. "It's going to be awfully hard to . . . it's going to be awfully hard . . ." she repeats, then is silent. She takes his hand between her two hands and kisses it, caresses it with her lips. "What's that music?" she asks.

"I think they're practicing something for the reconsecration of the church on Sunday," David replies.

"Let's say goodbye here and now. Andreas wanted you to come to dinner, but I said I thought you were engaged." David nods. "It's much better to say goodbye now, when we're by ourselves. To think it should be so hard. I don't think we realize how painful it's going to be *later*."

They sit in silence for quite a long time. Then she kisses him hastily. "I'll go now," she says.

"No, not yet, Karin."

"Yes, I'll go now. I must go now. Otherwise it will be too hard." She kisses him again.

14.

"David, dearest, I didn't think it was going to hurt so much being without you. It hurts physically. It's hard, too, not being able to show anything. I've no one to talk to. If only I had a friend I could tell everything to. Oh yes, I've women friends all right, but I don't trust them. It's got cold again here, almost like autumn, although we're well into May. We've all had bad colds, and I was absolutely streaming. Which was a good thing, really, as I cried so often to myself. I mean, I could go about legitimately with a red nose and red-rimmed eyes."

"Karin, my darling Karin. It feels odd to be back in the world. Your little town with its old wall and the silent streets and the cathedral with its chimes was outside reality in some way. Do you know what I mean? It was like a haven, far away from all evil. I felt comfy and safe. We've been separated now for six weeks and we've written to each other nearly every day. And I who am so bad at writing letters. One day I stopped dead in the street and said aloud to myself: 'We're painfully united.'"

"David, the dearest friend I have in the world. Can you forgive me for not writing to you for several days. We've had spring cleaning. I suppose you think that's a very trivial reason for not writing, but I haven't had a minute to myself from morning till night. The house has been full of people. Yes, it's been awfully hard work. Don't be cross with me. You see, it's hard sometimes not having anywhere to go where you can be by yourself."

"Karin, dearest. I'm now in the South of France at a sort of *summer congress for archaeologists. It's frightfully hot and we drag ourselves through an endless program of lectures and demonstrations and film shows. I've been told I can come back to Sweden on October 14. It's exactly ninety-six days until then. I check them off in my diary. It seems ages."*

"Dear, dear David. Now we're home from the country, and I must say I'm glad. The children have started school again and I've a little more time to myself. I'm going to learn Italian after all, that's today's big news. Otherwise, I spend a lot of time consoling Agnes, who has had her first broken romance. The heartache and the tears! Only seven weeks now until you come."

"Karin! Just a quick note. I've been able to rent our dingy, ugly old apartment! Am arriving on Thursday by air. I'll ring you on Friday morning at eight o'clock. It's really . . . I don't know what it is!"

15.

It's now eight o'clock Friday morning and the telephone is to ring. Karin is puttering about listlessly, sorting newspapers—those to be thrown out and those to be kept. Then she decides they're all to go. There are other things to be done. She goes down into the basement and loads the washing machine, stopping now and again to listen, but the telephone doesn't ring. The time now is seven minutes past eight. She lifts the telephone to hear whether it's working properly. It is. She sits down with her bills and begins writing out checks; at least she's near the telephone. It's now twelve minutes past eight. Then it rings. It's someone wanting the professor. Swallowing her disappointment, Karin replies politely that the professor is in his office at the hospital. "Oh, I see," the man says slowly and mournfully. "Then I suppose I can't get hold of him."

"You can speak to his secretary," Karin says. "She's sure to be able to help you."

"Yes, but I wanted a word with the professor himself," the man replies.

"He starts operating at eight o'clock, so I don't see how you can."

"Does he start operating?" the man exclaims in astonishment.

"Every day," Karin says. "Every day at eight o'clock."

"Saturdays too?" the man asks in surprise.

"No, not Saturdays."

"Who am I speaking to?" the man persists.

"It's his wife."

"Oh, I see . . . it was the professor I wanted to speak to."

"So I gather," Karin snaps.

"Goodbye then?" the mournful one suggests.

"Goodbye, take a chance on the secretary," Karin says, trying to smooth things over.

She puts the phone down and stares at it in fury. It is now sixteen minutes past eight. Karin decides to ring up instead. A recorded voice refers her to the exchange. She dials the given number and is told that the subscriber's number is cut off. Almost immediately it rings again. This time it's David.

"At last," he says, "I thought I'd never get through. I'm at a café around the corner. I didn't know that that goddamn phone was cut off. How are you?"

"Fine, I'm fine," Karin stammers, quite unable to think.

"Well, here I am anyway," David says with a sudden edge to his voice.

"Perhaps we could meet," Karin suggests after an anxious little pause.

"Not at all a bad idea," David replies with a mirthless laugh. "What about this afternoon? I have to meet a couple of people at two o'clock, but I'll be free by four-thirty."

"Can't you manage earlier?" Karin asks. "It'll be so short. I must be home for dinner, you see. We'd have less than an hour."

"Let's wait till tomorrow then," he says offhandedly.

"No, no! I didn't mean that," Karin says quickly.

"What are you doing now?" he asks suddenly.

"Now?" Karin replies. "I've just switched on the washing machine and I have to meet Anders's teacher at ten o'clock."

"Come *now*," David says.

"I can't," Karin gasps out anxiously. "I can't, it's impossible. I can't just drop everything."

"Come just for a bit. Then we can meet properly tomorrow." The telephone starts crackling in a disturbing way.

"I'll come," Karin says desperately. "I'll come at once."

"It's as filthy as hell up in the apartment," David says. "I don't think anyone has cleaned there for six months."

"It doesn't matter. I'll come now."

Putting the phone down, she looks about her in the familiar room, which suddenly seems so strange to her. She puts on her coat and hunts for the car keys. She looks at herself quickly in the mirror and checks her movement: a strange woman. A strange woman in a strange room on her way to a strange man, and not knowing where that way is leading her. "What am I doing? I'm crazy," she says to herself.

There is a thick mist and the streets of the little town are almost empty. She parks in the familiar sidestreet around the corner. On the stairs there is the same stench of damp and cats. She rings the doorbell. He opens at once. He seizes her hand and pulls her into the dark hall and shuts the door. Now they are standing facing each other, anxious and tense.

"How thin you've got," she says.

"I've been ill recently," David replies. "But I'm better now."

"I haven't smoked one cigarette since you left," Karin says.

"That's why you're even prettier than before."

"I've put on weight and that's not at all good."

They are still standing in the room. Suddenly she smiles and kisses him, grasping his hand and laying it against her breast inside the coat. She pulls him down onto the grubby bedspread. "Lie down on top of me," she says. He throws his arms around her and lies on top of her, kissing her again and again, slowly and searchingly. Then they help one another with their clothes, which drop all around them, and as he thrusts into her she murmurs: "It's worth everything."

16.

David and Karin lie in the twilight of an autumn afternoon. The doorbell rings. David says it's probably his assistant who promised to bring some books. He gets up and puts on his dressing gown. Karin continues to lie in the darkness of the bedroom, dozing. David opens the door. Andreas gives an embarrassed smile and asks if he may come in. David hesitates for a second, then nods. Andreas goes through the little hall into the living room.

"Can we have a light on?" he says. David turns on the ceiling light, which at one time has been covered by a shade; now it is merely a naked bulb. "Do you mind if I sit down for a moment?" Andreas asks. "I won't be long-winded." He sits down and takes off his glasses; he is fatigued and bewildered. "People are so kind," he says, with a faint smile. "I have received a couple of letters. This is a small town, you see. Everyone knows everyone else." He puts a letter on the table. "Anonymous, of course," he adds, smiling again. "Naturally I wouldn't take any notice of these poison pens if I didn't think they were telling the truth. I don't really know why I came. It was on the spur of the moment, I admit, but I felt it was necessary. One seldom knows exactly why one does things, hm?"

"I have nothing to say," David replies coldly.

Karin watches the two men in the brightly lighted room. She herself is more or less hidden by the gloom of the bedroom.

"No, I've really nothing to say," David repeats. "I hate so-called scenes. Anyway, I always think it's pointless discussing feelings. It's only idle supposition for the most part. I don't understand why you've come to see me. It seems as if you imagined you had rights of some kind. Karin says she feels a strong loyalty to you and your marriage. I think you ought to be grateful for that loyalty and hope it will survive this affair of Karin's and mine. I think you'd better talk to Karin. I think you should take advantage of her loyalty. I think you should make yourself touching and helpless. I think you should talk about the children and about all your years together. You have the upper hand, Andreas. Don't worry."

"I didn't come here to talk about myself," Andreas says. "I'm quite sure of that. I think I came to talk to you about Karin, though that may be a rationalization."

"Well, how touching," David says, with a laugh. "What are you going to tell me about Karin that I don't already know? Go now, Andreas. You've humiliated us long enough with this ridiculous visit."

"I don't really know who you are," Andreas says slowly, remaining seated. "I don't know you. Actually, I like you. I liked you from the outset, when I took charge of you at the hospital after your attempted suicide."

"It wasn't an attempted suicide," David retorts coldly. "It was an accident with that confounded gas stove."

"I don't think my memory is at fault," Andreas says with some surprise. "During our talk on that Tuesday night you yourself described your accident as an attempted suicide. Am I wrong?"

"No, but we were never to speak of it."

"That's true, forgive me," Andreas says, with a quick smile. "Forgive me. I didn't mean to be offensive or indiscreet. Anyway, what does it matter? What I wanted to say was that I liked you. We seemed to respond to each other. My feelings on that point have not changed."

"Have you anything else, anything more to say?" David asks, breaking a short silence.

"I don't believe that habit, marriage, and children are any firm shield against the outside world," Andreas answers wearily.

"The outside world," David repeats ironically.

"Call it what you like," Andreas says. "Erotic attraction or sexual obsession or emotional confusion or fear of a void or perhaps simply boredom. I don't know. It was stupid of me to come." He gets up and goes to the door. "If you think I intend putting an ultimatum to Karin, you're wrong. Nor do I intend any emotional blackmail. I don't intend doing anything, in fact. Karin must make up her own mind. That will be difficult enough. She hates any form of decision."

Andreas says goodbye politely and shuts the door carefully behind him. David sits down on a chair, laughing to himself. Karin dresses in silence.

"Wasn't that touching," David says. "That was just too goddamn touching. That was as touching as hell."

"Do you think he knew I was here?"

"Of course he knew, he's not such a fool."

Karin sits down opposite David and looks at him, takes his hand between hers, shakes her head, kisses him on the cheek and on the lips. "Will you call me tomorrow morning as usual?" she asks gravely.

"I don't know," David replies irritably.

"Do as you like," Karin says calmly, getting up to go.

"This situation is impossible," David says. "It's insufferable, isn't it?"

"Have you any suggestions?" Karin asks, still grave.

"I behave like a spoiled child," David says. "Don't I? Like a horrid, fretful little child. Don't I?"

"That's exactly what you do," Karin says. "But no one expects anything else of you."

Suddenly David starts to laugh. Stretching his arms above his head, he laughs loud and disconsolately. Then he holds out his hand and draws her to him and kisses her so that it hurts. She complains loudly, but returns the kiss. He lays his hand on her breast. "It's strange that such a hopelessly childish notion can go on existing through the years without the slightest encouragement but accompanied by any number of disappointments. Do you want to know what I mean?" He smiles despairingly at her. *We shall never get inside each other.* I shall never be able to disappear in you. You can never live inside me. It's only for short, hopelessly short moments that we imagine the prison has been opened. It's not true, it's only one lie among all the other lies. Do you know what I think? I think it's some dim memory from the womb. That's the only fellowship there is, and then that's the end for ever and ever amen." He laughs and gets up. "Now we deserve a drink. Don't we?"

"I must go, really," Karin says.

"Do you understand what I mean?" David asks, rummaging for a bottle and a couple of glasses.

"I understand what you mean," Karin replies, with a smile. "But I think it's just a lot of talk."

"Exactly!" David exclaims. "Exactly! It's just talk. Karin knows better!"

Karin goes up to him and puts her arms around him, pressing her forehead to his shoulder. "Why must it be like this?" she says miserably in her own language. "I don't think I can go on much longer. Why must it be so difficult?"

"Talk so that I understand," David says gently. "You sound so miserable."

"Not at all," Karin says. "It's worse than that."

"Don't go!" he says in sudden anguish. "Don't go now. I know what it will be like. You'll get home and everything will be the same. The children will want you to share their troubles, you'll help Anders with his homework, and Agnes will be lovesick and want you to console her. And then you'll cook the dinner and Andreas will tell you what sort of day he's had at the hospital. Then someone will ring up and ask you both to dinner on Friday of next week. And then you'll watch TV and talk for a while and then you'll go to bed and you'll fall asleep with Andreas' hand in yours. I know how it is. I know. I want you to stay here with me tonight. I want you to ring home to Andreas and say you can't come. I want you to. He must understand and accept. He can't have all the rights on his side."

"I've no idea how it will go. Perhaps we'll quarrel. Perhaps we'll get tight. Or perhaps we'll behave like a respectable bourgeois man and wife. We may even go out and have dinner and go to a movie."

"But surely you can stay with me just this one evening and night."

Karin is standing in the middle of the floor in the harsh light. She stands quite still, with eyes closed and head bent. "No," she says. "No, it's no good. You can't force me. If you force me and I stay, I won't be here anyway. And I'll find it hard to forgive you—afterward. It's better that I go."

"I understand," David says gently. "I understand although I don't understand. Forgive me for asking it of you."

Suddenly Karin steps to the telephone and dials a number. Andreas answers. Karin says: "Andreas, I'm staying with David this evening and tonight."

17.

That night Karin can't sleep. David is lying on his back with his hands on his chest. His breathing is almost inaudible, his face is sallow and lugubrious, his mouth shut tight. Silently, cautiously, she gets out of bed, takes her clothes, and tiptoes into the other room, where she switches on the light and dresses hurriedly.

When she gets home she sees at once that the light is on in Andreas' study. She goes slowly upstairs and stops in the doorway. Andreas lifts his head and takes off his glasses. He is sitting at the desk but has no work in front of him.

"Are you working?" Karin asks.

"No," Andreas replies. "I was just sitting, actually. I found it hard to go to bed."

Karin hides her face in her hand. Andreas goes over to her. She begins to sob violently. She frees herself but doesn't move away. Once again he puts his arm around her shoulders. "Come, let's walk a little," he says. And they begin to walk up and down in the dark room.

18.

Karin is shopping with her daughter, Agnes, who needs a new winter coat. Karin sees him at once outside the shop window. He has caught sight of them; now he stands there waiting. He has just come from work, still has his overalls on and is dirty and unshaven. He has parked his old car in the middle of a pedestrian crossing. Karin tries to prolong the visit to the shop, but he won't go. At last Agnes notices him and draws her mother's attention. They don't buy a coat; Karin says she will think it over. Taking her daughter by the hand, they leave the shop. It is late afternoon and a lot of people are hurrying past. David intercepts them and puts out his hand to Agnes.

"Hallo, Agnes, how are you? I thought that green coat was very nice, why didn't you buy that? May I speak to your mother for a moment?" Agnes gives him a contemptuous look and walks over to a shop window.

"We can't stand here," Karin says, acutely embarrassed.

"No, of course not, I see that. I must see you. When can I talk to you?"

"We can meet at the church tomorrow afternoon at three o'clock. Let me go now."

David smiles wanly. He touches her, grabs her arm, holds her. Karin shakes her head.

"Let me go now."

He releases her at once and is gone.

Karin goes over to Agnes, who is gazing sulkily in a shop window at ladies' shoes. "Well, see anything you like?" Karin asks.

"It's beyond me how you can talk to that drip. He's just *too horrid!*"

"No, he's not," Karin replies.

19.

It is a rainy day in late winter. The church is closed, but David and Karin have borrowed the key at the vicarage. The interior of the church is murky and raw. They go up to the image of the Virgin and look at it for a while. David breaks their silence. "I heard that something peculiar has happened, something that no one can properly explain. Before she was walled up she was the home of some insect not known today. The larvae have been sleeping inside her in the dark for five hundred years. Now they have waked up and are eating the image away from within. No known insecticide has the slightest effect on the destructive creatures. Actually, they're beautiful. At any rate, as beautiful as the image itself."

They stand again in silence watching a strange little insect, which is creeping from the Virgin Mary's breast up toward her face. "Look," David says, "here on the child there's a whole cluster of them hibernating. It's not certain that she can be saved."

They are tense and hostile, remote from each other, disappointed and anxious. They grope for each other with hands and with kisses, but they can't find their way across the distance. "It's cold in here," Karin says. They look at each other mutely. "You're trying the whole time to force me," she says after a while. "It's too much for me. I've lost my footing or whatever it is. I used to be fairly secure in my world. Now I'm insecure at home and insecure with you." She speaks quickly and softly as if she were ashamed. "I can't be without you. Everything circles around you—you're there the whole time. I can't understand it. You're like my newborn child. At the same time you're an awful menace. If I were free I'd go with you anywhere. It's true, David. I'd do anything at all to make you happy.

No, quiet now, let me try and tell you how it is, it's so hard to explain.

"I *understand* how you think. I *understand* what it is that torments you. I *know* why you're forcing me and it makes me furious, but it only binds me to you all the more firmly. I wonder if there's something wrong with me because I feel like this.

"Yes, go on, laugh. But let me tell you something: *I know that you're going to leave me.* Isn't it odd? I can see it quite clearly. And I know it's getting closer and closer. I think you're fond of me almost in the same way as I'm fond of you. *Even so, you're going to leave me.* I know why. You hate yourself and therefore you hate me somewhere. There's a bit of you that wants to kill and destroy. You hate yourself because you think you've always betrayed people and let them down. Yes, it's true, David, that's what you think about yourself and you hate yourself for it. You will never forgive yourself, and you have no God who can forgive you. Nor a mother who can take you in her arms and forgive you. From the outset you thought I was a mother who would make you forget whatever it is that torments you. But no woman in the world can play that part for you.

"I feel so terribly sorry for you and I try to reach you, I'm trying the whole time to reach you, dearest David. But I know that you're getting further and further away from me, and it hurts so. I just want to scream and weep.

"No, wait, I've more to say, I've thought this over very carefully. What was I going to say now? Oh yes, now I know: I don't understand what's happening in the world. I don't read newspapers or look at TV, I hardly ever have time. Agnes has already started to scold me for not keeping up with the times. I don't believe in God, but the cruelty around me frightens me; I hate violence, I am mortally humiliated when you strike me. I believe only in one rule: I believe you should try to be kind and good, I believe you should try to avoid hurting other people. I don't believe life has any particular meaning, no, I don't. All the same, I've always liked living. I'm no idealist. I'm rather scared of all big words. I think you should be sensible, and I'm going to try and be sensible, even now, though it's almost impossible.

"You can never change me, except on the surface. No, that's not true either. You *have* changed me, through and through. But you can't change my thoughts and my common sense. And I know the terrible truth—*You will leave me.*

"It's hard to live two lives. Sometimes I find it almost impossible, but I know that it can be done and I know that Andreas would accept it, as he has already become rather tired and rather old. Yes, it's true. It *is* possible to live two lives, and perhaps slowly combine them into one wise and good life which would benefit other people and make them happy. But there's no living with your self-hatred, David. It's a fatal disease. It's a tumor which just grows and grows. I can't do anything about it, however much I like you and however hard I try. Do you understand me, David? I wonder why life should be so difficult. Why there's so much distance and so many kinds of loneliness. Why there's so much longing and so much hopelessness. Why it should be so implacable."

She looks at David with a completely bare face, no tears, almost no expression. "I'm cold," she says suddenly. "Can't you put your arms around me?" He does so. "Say something to me, something kind." But David shakes his head. No, he can't say anything. He is battling with a wordless rage which almost gets the better of him. "Say that you like me, at least," Karin says. But he is silent.

"I can feel that you're angry with me. Yes, you are. Look at me, David. Be angry with me if you like, as long as you don't leave me. I don't know what I'm going to do if I haven't got you." She caresses his face over and over again. "I'm here with you. We're together. That's all that matters."

The gray light of late winter is sinking; it gets restless and unsteady. They have to hunch their shoulders against the wind that buffets them outside the church door. The door bangs with a hollow echo. There is not a soul in sight. The snow has begun whirling through the dusk. Tears spring to Karin's eyes. The clouds sweep low across the sky. The heart breaks with longing, with loneliness. The mother's eyes are quite clear, childlike, and so desperately tormented. The hand with the wedding rings: what is to be done. "If only I could reconcile myself in time to the boundaries and the cruelty. Cruelty, the unintentional, overpowering cruelty."

David looks at Karin. "I wasn't allowed to, I couldn't show affection; all this about contact and closeness, it's the only thing that matters, the only thing that assuages anguish and rage. The only thing that alleviates exposure in the world."

He checks her and says her name over and over. The gap between them disappears, the hatred and fear subside. Sudden reprieve for a short moment. This is you. I recognize you. I can comprehend you. They meet and blend into one another, ceasing to explain or to understand. In this twilight winter wasteland, they are shivering and with wet faces.

"Forgive me," he says. "Forgive me, forgive me, Karin. We are with each other now, aren't we? Now, at this moment."

Karin says, "Yes, yes, now we are with each other." And for a short moment it is so.

"You're not running off with the keys of the church, are you?" the vicar calls anxiously as he comes puffing up the slope.

20.

This meeting has happened just a few days before Easter; now it is Wednesday. David does not phone when he said he would, at eight o'clock in the morning. As so often before, Karin waits for the telephone bell with growing uneasiness and irritation, unable to get going with the day's duties. What is more, Anders is at home, feigning illness to get out of going to school. He has been sent to do his homework and sits grumbling over his arithmetic. About half-past eight Karin calls David's number; there is no answer. She calls a second time to make sure she hasn't dialed the wrong number. No answer.

Suddenly all the safety catches give way. With rising panic she drives down to the museum. It is still shut, but she goes in by the office entrance. She recognizes one of the assistants and asks for David.

"Wasn't he to be at the museum today?"

"Oh yes, they have a big sorting job on hand." He shows her a long worktable cluttered with plastic bags and various objects. "But he's usually a bit late. Can I give him a message?"

"No, it doesn't matter, I'll phone him later."

"We'll be here all afternoon," the assistant says, smiling politely.

"Oh, good," Karin says abstractedly. "I was going to ask him to dinner," she adds.

"I see," the assistant says. "David's an extremely nice person."

Karin does not answer this; she gives a quick nod and goes.

She unlocks the door to the apartment with her own key. It is empty and silent. David has packed and left. He is gone. She sits for a long time on the bed, looking out the dirty window. Out there is a line of gray windows opposite with their black spaces. In here is the unmade bed; the armchair with the sagging springs. He has forgotten his slippers; they are lying abandoned over by the table. The kitchen is a mess. He has left in a hurry. She looks about her. No letter, no message. The keys are lying on the table in the living room. A physical pain begins to spread through her limbs, a smarting in the eyes, a difficulty in breathing.

She opens the drawer of the desk. There lie the photographs she has given him, and also the letters she has written and her small scribbled messages. It is quite a big bundle. She goes into the kitchen and fills a glass with water. She drinks thirstily, but it doesn't ease the pain. She lets the glass drop on the hard surface of the draining board. The water splashes up, the splinters lie there sharp and enticing. She cuts her hand, sees the blood ooze up in her palm. It gives a moment's relief.

21.

At lunchtime Karin goes to see her husband at the hospital. His office is high in the huge building. In the secretary's room diligence and order prevail. (The secretary is a pretty young woman, very well-groomed, very obliging, very impersonal.) She thus feels it her duty to make polite conversation to her boss's wife while Karin is waiting for Andreas. She starts with the children; she herself has a little daughter. She says what a lot of sickness there has been during this long winter—everybody has been ill—then relates that she had found snowdrops in the bed by the south wall of the house. She asks politely whether Karin has had any snowdrops yet. Yes, she has. Then, frowning suddenly, the secretary says in a worried tone that the professor takes on far too much work; this big report about the new neurological clinic entails a tremendous amount of extra work. And Doctor Backman, taking sick leave like that. She doesn't call that loyalty, no certainly not.

Andreas comes in quickly, and gives Karin a welcoming smile, which vanishes the moment he sees her face. He exchanges a few words with the secretary. "I only want to speak to you for a few minutes," Karin says in a disciplined way.

"I see," Andreas says. "Please ask Jacobi to come this afternoon instead and then we can have a proper talk. Anyway I'm damned tired."

"Jacobi at five-thirty, is that convenient?"

"Yes, that's fine," Andreas replies, holding open the door to the inner room.

"Then I'll go to lunch now," the secretary says.

"Yes, do," Andreas says with a nod.

They are alone in the inner office, which is large and handsomely, but impersonally, furnished. Andreas takes off his shoes. "You don't mind if I talk to you lying down, do you," he asks, lying on the sofa and putting a cushion behind his head. "I have a confounded headache."

Karin sits down at the desk. "What is it you want to say? Obviously it's something unpleasant," Andreas says with a pitiful attempt at a smile.

"I must go to London," Karin says. "I know I shouldn't go. But it's like this: David has left me. I must find him. I must talk to him. He must tell me *why* he has left me. Try to understand me."

"I do *not* understand you," Andreas says calmly. "I will not countenance your rushing off headlong to a foreign country in search of your lover. There's a limit to what I can tolerate. I think you have exceeded the limit. If you go, you need not come back. If, on the other hand, you stay at home and try to get over your panic, I promise to help you in every way."

"I only want to go for a couple of days."

"You hear what I say. If you go, there is no way back. It's very simple. If you don't go, we'll help each other sort it all out and try to clear up this distressing, incredible thing."

"Just for one day, Andreas. I beg of you. Be fair."

"Don't you talk to me about fairness," Andreas retorts with a sudden flash of hatred. "Don't come crying to me for consideration or sympathy. Take your responsibility and bear it. Make your decision, Karin. And take the consequences *for once*."

Andreas sits up, he is pale and has deep gray shadows under his eyes. He looks at her with a steady, calm contempt. "This little drama has been going on for nearly two years. Now I'm tired of it. I don't want to be in another act."

Karin looks at her husband without averting her eyes. For a brief moment she senses the sweetness of the final catastrophe.

"Suffering must have an end, Karin. It can't go on indefinitely. I refuse to be poisoned by hatred and spite. I don't want to hate you."

"I must go," Karin says quietly.

"So it seems," Andreas says calmly. "We'll have to settle up the practical consequences when you return. Are you going to tell the children, or shall I?

"It's better you do."

"I'd be glad if you'd go now," Andreas says wearily. And she goes.

22.

Now Karin is standing at the passport control window at London airport. The immigrations officer asks her what she's going to do in England. She's at a loss for an answer, as she was not expecting the question.

"I don't know," she replies. "I'm going to meet some people."

"What sort of people?" the man asks in a bored way. "Friends?"

"I'm here as a tourist," Karin answers.

"Oh, tourist visit," the man says, relieved, adding: "Why didn't you say so?"

She checks in at a huge, shabby hotel right in the center of town and is stuck into a wretched, dingy little room at the very end of a long, dirty corridor. The window opens onto a brick wall which is so close that she could touch it. She has a bath, changes, and goes down into the street.

It is a sultry spring evening. A violent thunderstorm looms in black and yellow clouds over the city. Sunday—the gray chasms of the empty streets, distant churchbells. A dance palace switches on its neon sign in the thundery dusk. Behind the pillars and on the steps some emaciated girls and boys are lounging in extraordinary clothes. They stand half-hidden, looking like bluish specters, not talking to each other.

Karin hails a taxi, which takes her to the right address. It's an endless residential area with tallish, dilapidated, and neglected houses stretching down dirty red streets in long lines. Here and there clusters of children play football; they scatter screeching like hungry birds. Another churchbell is ringing, but there is the same leaden, thundery sky, the same dream, the same unalleviated anguish.

She goes up four flights of stairs; there's no name on the door. She knocks.

A woman opens the door. She is rather short, with large breasts and hips under a tight-fitting, unbecoming Sunday dress. Her eyes are blue and childish. Her face is childishly round and the mouth broad with bitter corners.

"Does David live here?" Karin asks at once.

The woman nods: "Yes, he lives here, but he's not at home."

"Can I wait for him?"

"I don't think he'll be home today."

Karin looks away, unable to meet the other woman's eyes; she is now very tired.

"Won't you come in and sit down for a while?" the woman asks in a friendly tone. "My name's Sara," she adds, smiling. "You're Karin, I know."

Karin goes into the apartment, which consists of two rooms and a kitchenette. There is hardly any furniture, and no pictures on the walls. The two women sit down on either side of the stained, rickety table. Sara offers Karin a glass of brandy, which she gratefully accepts.

"Are you his wife?" Karin asks.

Sara bursts out laughing, as if the question were comic. "I'm his sister," she says. "I keep house for him."

"He told me he didn't have any relations."

Sara shrugs, and picks at a broken tooth. "Would you like something to eat?" she asks. "I've some sausage and cheese in the house. I can make you a couple of sandwiches if you're hungry."

"No, thank you," Karin says. "No, thank you. It's very kind of you, but I'm not hungry."

The two women regard each other in silence.

"Are you going to have a baby?" Sara asks. Karin nods. "Whose is it?" Sara asks again. "Is it David's child or your husband's?"

"Does it matter?" Karin says.

"Why are you pregnant?" Sara demands.

"I don't know. It seems rather funny, doesn't it?"

"Not to me," Sara says, draining her glass. Karin looks at her hands: Sara is holding the glass in a crooked and clumsy grip. Sara notices her glance. "You're looking at my hands, aren't you? It's muscular paralysis. Atrophy. It runs in the family and apparently can't be explained scientifically. David also suffers from it, though not so noticeably. It affects the hands and feet." She gives a little smile and says in David's tone of voice: "What shall we do now? Shall we talk about David?"

"Suppose you tell me about yourself," Karin says. She has begun to feel sick and a vague dread is clutching at her.

Sara shakes her head. "I don't think that can interest you."

"Well, you *are* David's sister," Karin says lamely.

"Yes, exactly, we have everything in common, at any rate over the last few years." Sara smiles. "We're inseparable."

"Are you married?" Karin asks.

"I lost my husband in the Six Day War. David studied at the university in Tel Aviv. When he had passed his exams he cleared out of the country. I think it was mean of him." She pours out what is left in the bottle. "When I was left alone I looked David up here in London. As I said, we're inseparable, David and I. He says that he's never going to leave me. If you know what I mean." There is silence, then a quick anxious glance: "You understand, don't you?"

Karin gets up. "Thank you, I'll go now."

"Will you come back tomorrow?"

"No, I don't think I'll come back."

They say goodbye.

Karin stops in the street. When she looks up at the house, Sara can be glimpsed at the window.

Later Karin is sitting quite still in her hotel room. The evening light is sinking, and the street lamps cast reflections on the ceiling and walls. She hears strange voices and footsteps in the corridor. A woman laughs and gives an excited scream in the room above. Somewhere there is dance music. She sits with her hands clasped in her lap, looking out the window. The hours pass. Now and then she weeps quietly; the tears start to flow, then she gives a dry little sob and sighs. She dries her tears. They come again. Evening turns to night.

23.

It is early autumn, the beginning of September. Karin and Agnes are sitting together at the big kitchen table. Between them is a huge basket filled to the brim with apples from the garden. They are busy peeling them and cutting them up. The sun is shining brightly and the windows are open. Karin's pregnancy is now far advanced. They work is peaceable silence.

"I'd like to ask you something," Agnes says.

Karin nods: "By all means." But no question comes. Agnes is intent on peeling a large apple. "Well, what did you want to ask me?"

"I want to know if you really intended to go off and leave us and Daddy last spring when you went to London. Were you going to clear out and leave us and live with that David?"

Karin is given a short respite: Anders stamps through the kitchen calling for a Band-Aid or any damned thing; he has fallen off his bike and hurt his knee. The repair is carried out, calm is restored, and Anders disappears.

"You forgot to answer my question," Agnes says, going on with the peeling and slicing.

Karin thinks for a moment, puts down the knife and wipes her hands on her slacks. "I don't know what to say," she answers. "I never thought of you and Anders and Daddy. I didn't think at all."

"I just don't understand it," Agnes snorts, a note of contempt in her voice.

"No," Karin says. "I don't expect you to understand something I don't understand myself."

Karin's hands are busy. Her mind is rich in memories and experience. She has borne two children and is soon to give birth to another one, which she longs for and desires. She knows everything about her daily life. It gives her constant duties; she surveys them and carries them out with wisdom and a practiced hand. She feels no tedium or tiredness. The mere fact of living is a matter of course to her. She doesn't ask, doesn't accuse. The days pass, one very much like another; it doesn't frighten her. She matures, she gathers knowledge. For a short period of her life she was afflicted with a severe fever, which forced her to act in a strange way, to make peculiar decisions, to bring about suffering. Then she returned in humility to her familiar reality and tried to make amends for the wrong she considered she had done.

"It was hardest for Daddy," Karin says, looking steadily at Agnes.

24.

Just before dusk on a gray, rainy afternoon in early winter, Karin is on the way to her Italian lesson and takes the short cut through the botanical garden, which is now bare and leafless. Her pregnancy is now very far advanced, but she nevertheless moves with ease.

She sees him while still some distance away. He is waiting for her at the agreed rendezvous: the bridge over the stream that flows through the park. He is bareheaded and is wearing an old raincoat; he stands looking down into the water. When he catches sight of her he goes toward her at once, tries to embrace her, but she moves quickly aside, not daring to look him in the eyes.

"Why do we have to meet in this idiotic place?" David asks roughly. "Let's go to my hotel."

"No," Karin says. "No, I don't want to. I can only spare five minutes. I'm on the way to my Italian lesson. It starts at four o'clock.

We can meet here without anyone seeing us. I've had enough scandals. It never occurred to you that this is a small town."

"Nor to you," David answers, with a smile. "I did think of it, but I didn't care."

They stand silent, at a loss for something to say. Karin begins, "Let's walk, I'm feeling cold, this is the worst time of year, so nasty and raw."

"Yes, if you like," David says wearily, starting to walk beside her. They are silent again.

"You wanted to talk to me," Karin says. Her tone is formal, though she doesn't really mean it to be.

"You wanted to talk to me," David mimics, and laughs.

"Just what do you expect?" Karin asks, turning toward him. "You suddenly turn up, God knows where from, call me up in the middle of dinner, and say you must see me, it's terribly important, and I must come to your hotel. You must be out of your mind. You've no right to come here making demands." She looks at him anxiously. David says nothing, his eyelids twitch.

"I've tried living without you," he says after a while. "I thought it would be possible. I thought I could go back to my old life. I can't. It hurts physically being without you. It's like a constant ache; whatever I do I can't get away from it. I didn't know it was going to be like this. I didn't know I was so terribly tied to you. I thought I'd get over it. When I left you it was to be spared more feelings, tears, scenes. I'd had enough. I wanted to make a clean break. I wanted to have peace at last. But it didn't turn out that way. It just got worse. I can't live without you. It sounds so utterly ridiculous to say, 'I can't live without you.' But it's true. I can't express it in any better way. Everything has changed, I don't know what has happened, I can't understand it. I'm no longer the same person, I think and react and feel differently. In the old days, before I met you, I could live without living, I didn't care, nothing mattered anyway."

She shakes her head. "Don't say any more, David. It makes it so hard."

He grows suddenly matter-of-fact. "Listen now, Karin. I've been offered an associate professorship at the University of Århus. We could live a settled life on your conditions. You can bring the children, everything will be the way you want. You'll have your security. I'm not going to rush you any more. I don't mean you have to make up your mind at once. I can wait. I'll be patient."

"I don't care about security anymore," Karin says swiftly. "I don't bother about it because I know there isn't any security except what you create from inside yourself." She has nothing more to say. "Goodbye, David. You must let me go now. There's no point in this. We've nothing more to talk about."

"You can't just leave me like this," David bursts out, taking her roughly by the arm as though to stop her. "Please, don't go!"

She suddenly looks at him. "Poor David. I love you so much. I love you."

"It's not true!"

"Yes, it is true. It's the truth. No one has done me so much harm as you. No one has done me so much good. All the same, I'm not coming with you, David. It will probably torment me for the rest of my life. I know it's always going to hurt."

"You must have strong reasons if it's as you say," David says with sudden sarcasm.

"For me they are strong reasons. For you they're poor reasons, I know. For you they're perhaps not reasons at all." She looks away, then, plucking up courage, she says softly and quickly: "I feel it's my duty to stay where I am. It may be self-deception, but I don't think so. I *want* to be with you, *everything in me wants to be with you*. I can leave everything. I'm not afraid any more. Perhaps if Mother were alive it might be different. I don't know. But I feel it's my duty to stay here, so I will."

He grips her by the arms. "I know you're lying. They're just excuses. You don't mean what you say. I know the real reasons. They're so goddamn rotten and trivial and cowardly I can't be bothered going into them. Can't you see the pattern, Karin!"

Karin doesn't answer, she has closed her eyes, shut her face and her body. After a moment or two he lets her go so violently that she loses her balance and stumbles to one side. She stands unmoving, her face turned away.

"I know you're lying," he repeats more calmly and in a cold tone. She doesn't answer, shakes her head. "I know you're lying, do you hear?"

As she still doesn't answer, he leaves her. It has started to rain. Awkwardly, she picks up the Italian textbooks she has dropped.

CRIES AND WHISPERS

My dear friends!

We're now going to make a film together. It will look different from our earlier works, and this script will also look different. We shall strain the medium's resources in a rather complicated way. More than usual, therefore, I must tell you what it is I'm after; then we can get together and talk over how we are to give shape to our problems, cinematographically and artistically.

As I turn this project over in my mind it never stands out as a completed whole. What it most resembles is a dark flowing stream: faces, movements, voices, gestures, exclamations, light and shade, moods, dreams. Nothing fixed, nothing really tangible other than for the moment, and then only an illusory moment. A dream, a longing, or perhaps an expectation, a fear, in which that to be feared is never put into words. I could go on indefinitely describing key and color, we shouldn't be any the wiser. We had better get started.

The scene is set in a stately home, half mansion, half manorhouse. It was built perhaps sometime in the eighteenth century to serve as a retreat for a distinguished gentleman's cast-off mistress—I don't know. In any case it is not too large and not too small. There is also an old, rather neglected park, aflame with autumnal splendor. It is all remote, still, a shade dismal at times.

The time is the turn of the century. The women's clothes are lavish, expensive, concealing and revealing. We needn't get caught up in exact dates; it is not the precise beginning of a new era, and can just as well be the 1880s or 1890s. The important thing is that the clothes, by their power of suggestion, are in accord with our demand for atmosphere. The same applies very much to the interiors; when constructing them, we must bear in mind the possibilities of creating the lighting conditions we desire: dawns which don't look like dusk, soft firelight, the mysterious indirect light on a day when it is snowing, the gentle radiance from an oil lamp. The torment of a bright, sunny autumn day. A solitary candle in the darkness of night and all the restless shadows when someone wrapped in a wide peignoir hurries through the big rooms . . .

At the same time it is important that our décor never be obvious. It should be flexible, enclosing, elusive, and present, evocative without being obtrusive. There is a peculiarity about it, however: all our interiors are red, of various shades. Don't ask me *why it must be so,* because I don't know. I have puzzled over this myself and each explanation has seemed more comical than the last. The bluntest but also the most valid is probably that the whole thing is something internal and that ever since my childhood I have pictured the inside of the soul as a moist membrane in shades of red.

Furniture, props, and other paraphernalia must be very exact, but we must be able to use them capriciously and just as they suit our purpose. But everything must be beautiful and harmonious. It must be the way it is in a dream: a thing is there because we desire it or need it, just for the moment.

There are four leading characters in the drama. Four women. I shall give a brief account of them, without any order of precedence.

AGNES is thought of as being the owner of the estate, having lived on there after the death of her parents. She has never brought herself to move away from it; she has belonged there since birth, and has let her life flow quietly and imperceptibly along, without any meaning or misfortune. She has vague artistic ambitions—dabbling in painting, playing the piano a little; it is all rather touching. No man has turned up in her life. For her, love has been a confined secret, never revealed. At the age of thirty-seven she has cancer of the womb and is preparing to make her exit from the world as quietly and submissively as she has lived in it. She spends most of the night and the day in bed—her large bed in her parents' handsome but cluttered bedroom. But she can still get up now and then, until the pain strikes her down. She complains little and does not think that God is cruel. In her prayers she turns to Christ in meek expectation. She is very emaciated, but her belly has swollen up as though she were in an advanced stage of pregnancy.

KARIN, her elder sister by two years, married money and moved to another part of the country. She soon found out that her marriage was a mistake. Her husband, who is twenty years her senior, is repulsive to her physically and mentally. She is the mother of five children, but nevertheless seems untouched by maternity and matrimonial misery. She presents an irreproachable façade and is considered stuck-up and reserved. Her loyalty to her marriage is unshakable. Deep down, under a surface of self-control, she hides an impotent hatred of her husband and a permanent rage against life. Her anguish and desperation never come to light except in her dreams, which torment her from time to time. In the midst of this tumult of bridled fury, she bears a gift for affection, devotion, and a longing for nearness. This large capital lies immovably shut in and unused.

MARIA is the youngest sister. She, too, is wealthily and securely married to a good-looking and successful man in a suitable social position. She has a daughter of five; she herself is like a spoiled child—gentle, playful, smiling, with an ever-active curiosity and love of pleasure. She is very much taken up with her own beauty and her body's potentialities for pleasure. She is completely lacking in imagination about the world in which she lives; she is sufficient unto herself and is never worried by her own or other people's morals. Her only law is to please.

ANNA is the maidservant in the house. She is about thirty. As a girl, she had a daughter, and Agnes looked after her and the child. This meant that Anna became very attached to Agnes. A silent, never-expressed friendship was established between the two lonely women. The child died at the age of three, but the relationship between Anna and Agnes endured. Anna is very taciturn, very shy, unapproachable. But she is ever-present—watching, prying, listening. Everything about Anna is weight. Her body, her face, her mouth, the expression of her eyes. But she doesn't speak; perhaps she doesn't think, either.

The basic situation when the film (or whatever we're going to call our project) begins is this: Agnes's disease has rapidly got worse and the doctor does not give her much longer to live. The two sisters (her only relatives) have come to her deathbed.

2.

The clocks in the gray dawn. They all have their personalities, their voices. In the vague, uncertain light they are rather extraordinary, almost obtrusive. They all strike, one after the other, and some mingle their chimes. The mantelpiece clock, with flute-playing shepherd, in Agnes's bedroom, is the only one not going. The fire has burned down in the fireplace, the oil lamp flickers and sighs, the eyes of the family portraits stare, round and indifferent, at the new day approaching doubtfully between the autumnal trees of the park.

Agnes's eyes are inflamed with insomnia and suppressed physical pain. She has been lying for an hour or two, fighting the agony. It's better to get up, move about, sit in a chair, perhaps dip into a book. Perhaps it would be better if the hands of the clock on the mantelpiece were allowed to move. It's harder when it is silent.

Agnes stands for a long time by the window; there is mist and drizzle against the pane. Everything out there in the park is merely a blurred outline. Then it occurs to her that she should perhaps write something in her diary. Tensing her body against the shooting pain, she rummages for the book in the drawer of the bedside table, opens it, and sits down at the fragile escritoire. After thinking for a while, she writes: "It is early on Monday morning and I'm in pain. My sisters and Anna are taking turns to sit up. Kind of them. I needn't feel so alone with the dark . . ."

The door between the bedroom and the drawing room is ajar. Out there Maria is sitting up—that is to say, she has dropped off into a sound sleep, sunk deep in the chair. Her face is like that of a child, the mouth half open, the features relaxed.

Agnes blows out the flickering lamp. Then she hears Anna's footsteps in the corridor. Anna walks through the dark dining room and puts a tray down on the table. Her thick hair is plaited in a pigtail; she is barefoot under the simple nightgown. Agnes gets into bed and lies on her side; it hurts less that way. She hears Anna whispering to Maria.

Now Karin comes into the drawing room. Agnes sees them through the rectangle of the door—three white-clad, gleaming figures in the autumn morning light. The servant makes up the fire, which has died down. Maria stretches in the chair and yawns. Karin stands in the doorway looking at Agnes, who pretends to be asleep. Maria gets up out of the chair and the warm rug in which she has wrapped herself. She walks over to a large mirror which is tilting out from the wall; it has panels of blurred glass, a marble ledge, and an ornamental gold frame. She stands before the mirror for a moment, turning her face toward her image and smiling quickly, then turns around irresolutely to Karin, as though wanting to be told what to do. But Karin is busy with her needlework and takes no notice of Maria. With a sigh, Maria decides to go to her room.

The scene just described has haunted me for over a year. At first, of course, I didn't know the names of the four women and why they were dressed in white dresses that flowed down to their feet, or why they moved about in a gray morning light in a room with red wallpaper. Time and again I have rejected this picture, refusing to make it the basis of a film (or whatever it is). But the picture has persisted, and slowly, reluctantly, I have identified it: Three women who are waiting for the fourth to die and who take turns to watch by her.

If I now write that the wind is stirring in the big trees outside the bedroom window and that the mist is beginning to move and that for a short moment the sun dyes the walls of the room a deeper shade—if I write this, then this time I mean

that we shall try to achieve this phenomenon in one way or an-
other. It is also important that the shadows of the windows'
squares light up and grow dim gently, almost imperceptibly.

Maria has lain down to rest in the room she had as a girl, in
which the sunlight is touching the furniture and figures of a doll's
house. A few large roses glow in a thin, transparent porcelain bowl.
Opposite the bed is a painting of her mother when young—dressed
in white, and with an open, searching gaze turned on the beholder.
Maria rocks on the verge between sleeping and waking.

Karin bends over her needlework. The sunlight reaches her from
the side, gliding into her eyes and in under the eyelids, dazzling and
hampering. She turns her head toward the light and lowers her
hands. The sun floats like a burning ball among the misty clouds.
Suddenly she begins to weep—not violently or distractedly; in fact,
it is nothing more than tears running down her cheeks.

Anna is sitting on the edge of the bed in her garret when the sun
suddenly touches her hair. Slowly she pulls off the white nightgown,
undoes the thick plait, and lets her hair stream over her shoulders.
Then she begins to comb it with listless movements. Her face is expressionless, impassive. On the rickety table is a bowl of apples and a
faded photograph of Anna with her dead daughter.

This is one of Anna's pleasant memories: In the drawing room
there is a big music box that plays old dance tunes. One day, a thunderstorm breaks over the house. Agnes puts on all the lights in the
drawing room. Agnes, Anna, and Anna's little daughter dance and
play together while the rain beats against the windows. Then they
build a house under the big dining table. There they are as close as
a single body, in common, shuddering enjoyment, undisturbed by
the violent storm. In this way, they forget their fear.

If only we could produce a proper thunderstorm for once! If we
could conjure up the heavy, strange half light. And the flashes
of lightning against the windows. Heavens above!

Agnes has fallen asleep at last; the pain has left her, her body
has grown numb, and the sunlight quivers for a few moments on the
big bed in which she lies, small and hunched up, her hands open.
Now and then a shudder passes through the thin body, almost like a
sob, but it is nevertheless at peace now, and the little clock with its
flute-playing shepherd measures the time undisturbed.

3.

It is difficult nowadays to depict suffering and death in words or pictures. Simulated death or make-believe suffering is apt to become indecent, obscene. If we nevertheless set about describing a deathbed in some detail, we do so not out of curiosity or to take pleasure in frightening ourselves and the spectators. We do so in order to have a firm, well-built foundation for the development of our project.

I picture Agnes sitting up in bed with a lot of pillows behind her back. Anna has brought her some gruel and is sitting by the bed. But Agnes has no appetite; she pushes the bowl away, as if the food nauseated her. Maria and Karin are in the outer room, standing by the window, talking quietly. Another window is open. Perhaps it is Sunday morning; a soft light fills the rooms. Agnes seems to hear something: It is a dog barking far away.

A large bird flies up silently out of the old oak. Then Agnes hears footsteps. She says straight out, and as yet with no fear, that someone is walking out there. The three women look at her inquiringly. She repeats: Someone is walking out there.

Suddenly the drawing-room door opens, and the doctor comes in with his black bag. He pays his respects to Karin and Maria, goes in to Agnes without bothering to shut the door behind him, sits down on the edge of the bed, and talks mumblingly to his patient. He examines her perfunctorily, feeling her swollen belly, taking her pulse, fingering the glands in her armpits. Agnes has bent her head against her chest and tries to hold the doctor's hand between her hands. The doctor is a man of about forty, with a sallow, well-shaped, but slightly bloated face. He hides his eyes behind a shining pince-nez. His hair is already gray. He is dressed in a crumpled and ill-fitting suit. His hands are large and soft, his voice well modulated, with a sarcastic tone.

Karin goes in to Agnes, and Maria accompanies the doctor to the front door. They stand in silence, rather at a loss, without saying goodbye. Maria smiles and looks at the man exhortingly. As he goes to open the door she quickly takes his hand and puts it to her mouth. Then she throws her arms around his neck and kisses him. They stagger against the wall in a passionate embrace.

"When can I come to you?" she says.

He shakes his head and frees himself.

4.

AGNES'S DIARY:

Mother is in my thoughts nearly every day. She loved Maria because they were so alike in every way. I was too like Father for her to be able to stand me. When Mother spoke to me in her light, excitable way, I didn't understand what she meant. I tried terribly hard, but never managed to please her. Then she would get impatient. She was nearly always impatient, mostly with Karin. I was sickly and puny as a child, but Karin was always being scolded, because Mother thought she was so clumsy and unintelligent. Mother and Maria, on the other hand, had so much to talk about. I often used to wonder what they were whispering and laughing about, and why they got on so well together. They always had little secrets, and they used to tease me and Karin.

I loved Mother. Because she was so gentle and beautiful and alive. Because she was so—I don't know how to put it—because she was so *present*. But she could also be cold and indifferent. When I used to come and ask her for affection, she would rebuff me and be playfully cruel, saying she hadn't time. Yet I couldn't help feeling sorry for her, and now that I'm older I understand her much better. I should like so much to see her again and tell her what I have understood of her ennui, her impatience, her panic and refusal to give up.

I remember once—it was autumn—I came running into the drawing room; I suppose I had something important to do (one always has at the age of ten). Then I saw Mother sitting there in one of the big chairs. She sat there in her white dress, quite still, looking out of the window with her hands resting on the table. She was leaning forward slightly in a peculiar, stiff way. I went up to her. She gave me a look so full of sorrow that I nearly burst into tears. But instead I began to stroke her cheek. She closed her eyes and let me do it. We were very close to each other that time.

Suddenly she came to herself and said, "Just look at your hands, they're filthy. Whatever have you been up to?" Then, overcome with affection, she took me in her arms and smiled at me and kissed me. I was dazzled by these riches. Just as suddenly, she began to weep and begged my forgiveness over and over. I didn't understand a thing; all I could do was hold her tightly until she freed herself. Her face changed and, giving her little laugh, she dabbed her eyes. "How ridiculous," was all she said, then she got up and left me with my tumult.

5.

It is an autumn night. Agnes is reclining in the big bed. Her eyes are closed and her forehead has beads of sweat on it. Her mouth is bitten and covered with sores. Now and then her body shudders with the constant pain. At the moment, however, she is dozing.

In the drawing room (with the door to the bedroom wide open), Karin is bending over her needlework. A fire is burning in the open fireplace. The oil lamp sheds its soft light over her face and hands. It is quite still. The clocks tick, conversing in low, gentle voices.

Karin puts down her needlework and fixes her eyes on the large Italian painting of St. Theresa in the sacred third stage of prayer.

Let us devote a little time to Karin: She is sitting at the table with her husband in the dining room, with its heavy furniture and dark-red, gilt-leather wallpaper. At this time, they are living in the old family house for a brief period. It is already evening and the thick window curtains are drawn. Tablecloth and solid silver gleam in the yellow light of the lamps.

Husband and wife are dressed in black. Perhaps it is Good Friday, or else they are in mourning for some deceased relative, or they may have been to an afternoon reception at the Ministry for Foreign Affairs. Anna—she, too, in black, servant black—stands in discreet attendance with lowered head, waiting to be told to serve the dishes.

Karin's husband is a good deal older; his face is lean, his mouth tight-lipped, his eyes are calm but piercing, his smile is amiable but sarcastic. His head shakes slightly. His hands are large, with long, blunt fingers, and are hairy. The short beard and the gray hair are well-trimmed.

Husband and wife dine in silence. This silence is charged with hatred—a mutual hatred that is almost tangible, without mercy or let-up. Neither of them has taken a deep breath of relief for the last fifteen years. You could almost speak of the loyalty of total hatred. They owe each other nothing.

She has broad wedding rings, in the Swedish fashion, and between them a couple of costly diamond rings. She is also wearing a rope of large, real pearls, and earrings of an old-fashioned shape. He has given her many presents of jewelry over the years.

As I said, they dine in silence, but it isn't just an ordinary, slack silence. And there's this, too: the slight shaking of his head. He now turns to Anna and asks her politely to serve him more of the fish; she hurries over with the dish, which has been keeping hot on the sideboard. He smiles and thanks her, at the same time asking his wife if she will keep him company, but she won't (a shake of the head). He smiles at this too, confirmingly: Let's see who can stick it out the longest. Who will be the first to fall in this grim and never-ending duel?

"What are you smiling at?"

"I'm not smiling."

"Shall we have coffee in the drawing room or shall we go straight to bed?"

"I don't want any coffee, thank you."

Her wineglass tips over, the thin bowl with its faint pattern breaks in splinters, and the wine spreads over the whiteness of the cloth. She gives him a frightened glance, but he pretends not to notice what has happened. He finishes his meal, wipes his mouth with studied care. Then he tosses the crumpled napkin onto the table and gets up.

"It's late, I suggest we go to bed."

He doesn't wait for her assent or refusal; why should he? Leaving the two women, he closes the door of his study silently behind him. Anna begins at once to clear away the dishes. When her back is turned, Karin picks up one of the small splinters of the wineglass and holds it between thumb and forefinger a moment. Yes, it is small and sharp, with needlelike points sticking out, rather like a star.

"It's nothing but a tissue of lies," she says quietly and distinctly and dispassionately. *"It's nothing but a tissue of lies."*

Beyond the bedroom is Karin's boudoir. She is sitting at the mirror and letting Anna undress her. From the black dress, from the jewelry, from the stays and panties and stockings and crisp linen, a woman's body detaches itself. It seems to grow and expand, freed from the weight and restriction of the clothes. Having put on her nightgown and peignoir, she stands in the middle of the room, at a loss. Anna looks at her. Karin turns toward the servant and says quietly, "Don't look at me. Don't look at me like that, I say." Then she raises her ring hand and strikes her hard on the cheek. Anna jerks up one shoulder, but her eyes don't waver.

"Forgive me," Karin says, frightened by the expression in the woman's eyes. "Forgive me." But Anna shakes her head: not this, not forgiveness.

"You can go," Karin says.

Anna bobs and withdraws, closing the door behind the curtain.

The little glass splinter with its sharp points is lying on the dressing table. Karin picks it up, sits on the stool, and pulls up her night-gown. Opening her legs wide, she carefully inserts the splinter in her vagina. She sits for a few moments leaning forward. Then she stands up and brushes the hair and the cold sweat off her forehead; her eyes are black and staring. "It's nothing but a tissue of lies," she says again in the same absent-minded, dispassionate voice. She opens the door to the bedroom.

Her husband turns toward her; he is wearing a full-length dress-ing gown and is standing with an open book in his hand and specta-cles on his forehead. She goes past him, pulls up the quilt, and bares her private parts.

"You're bleeding," her husband says in disgust. Then Karin smiles.

6.

In the drawing room, Karin smiles at the picture of St. Theresa at her devotions. It is a sarcastic, almost obscene smile. She resumes her needlework. Anna enters the room silently, Karin gets up at once, putting the needlework in a plaited basket that is standing beside her on small cane legs. She says something to Anna, goes over to the door, and looks at Agnes, who pretends to be asleep.

"I think she's asleep," Karin says, turning toward Anna.

Suddenly and vaguely, they sense the nearness of death. They look at each other in a moment of open fear. In this moment, they share the immobility of night, the stifling silence, the suffering face of the sick woman, faintly illuminated by the night light, the whis-pering voices of the clocks.

"I feel cold," Karin says to herself. Then she leaves the room.

Anna goes over to the oil lamp and turns down the wick until there is only a faint glow. She sits down so that she can see Agnes, drawing the dark shawl more closely about her.

Agnes opens her eyes and whispers something. She has to repeat it. "Come here, Anna! Come to me! You're so far away!"

Anna gets up at once and closes the door behind her. She stands at the foot of the bed.

"Come to me, be with me," Agnes murmurs.

Letting the shawl slip to the floor, Anna takes off her warm, thick stockings and snuggles down into bed. Then she opens her nightgown, baring her large breasts, and puts her arms gently around the sick woman, whispering inaudible words of comfort, cradling her, kissing her mouth and cheeks, holding her tight. Agnes sinks into her tenderness and grows calm; the hard tension in her tormented body softens and relaxes. "How good you are," she whispers. "You're so kind and good." Anna strokes the invalid's head and face with her large, moist hand. Then they fall asleep, embracing each other.

7.

About seven o'clock in the morning, in the fluid gray dawn, Agnes falls into a coma. Her breathing is deep and frightening, her mouth gapes as if she were suffocating, and her pulse is so feeble that it can hardly be felt. Her cheeks have dark-red blotches, while her lips turn blue and swollen. About nine-thirty, the deep breathing changes to violent convulsions, which twist the invalid's arms and legs. Her eyes half open and she mumbles slurringly. The symptoms of choking increase, and she flings herself forward as if a giant hand had seized her body, pressing it together.

After another hour or so, the attack passes and the tortured body relaxes. The face resumes its natural pallor. Her breathing now is almost inaudible. She asks for something to drink. Her lips are dry and bitten, her thin hair matted and damp with sweat. Anna and Karin help each other make up the bed with clean sheets. They wash the wasted body with warm water; they comb her hair and get her into a clean nightgown.

The doctor comes and carries out his quick examination. The invalid is given an injection of morphine and sinks into a light, restless sleep. The other women wait in the drawing room outside the bedroom, each thrown back on her own thoughts. About five o'clock in the afternoon, the sun breaks out like shimmering horizontal spear points. Those keeping vigil stare, dazzled and mute, into the hard, bright light. Agnes moans and the frightening deep breathing starts again. This time the convulsions are more violent. The body is flung to and fro in the bed. Suddenly she shouts: "Can't you help me? Help me, I don't want to! I don't want to!" She utters a piercing scream and beats about her with her arms until a new attack of choking cuts off her shrieks and she bends backward, mouth agape.

The doctor gives her another dose of morphine, but nothing helps. A gigantic force, which seems to come from without, shakes the racked body. A sudden vomiting spurts over the bed. She shouts over and over again, the words no longer distinguishable. Then she suddenly sinks down, deep down into the bed; her body trembles violently and her eyes open.

Maria begins to weep—perhaps it is the easing of the tension and fear. Karin passes one hand across her face as if to brush away a cobweb. Anna helps the doctor put the dead woman to rights. A window is opened. Agnes's eyes are closed and her hands laid over her breast. The sunlight fades slowly and imperceptibly; the big rooms are filled with a bluish light. No one has a mind to light candles. A mysterious calm has set in.

8.

Sometimes I want to cover my face with my hands and never take them away again. How am I to grapple with the loneliness? The long days, the silent evenings, the sleepless nights. Whatever am I to do with all this time that pours over me? Then I go into my despair and let it burn me. I've found that if I try to avoid it or shut it out, everything becomes much harder. It's better to open yourself outward, to accept what torments or hurts you. It's better not to shut your eyes or try to dodge it, as I did before.

When I write about loneliness, though, I'm being unfair. Anna is my friend and companion, and I think her loneliness is worse than mine. After all, I can console myself with my painting, my music, and my books. Anna has nothing. Sometimes I try to talk to her about herself, but it makes her shy and reticent.

9.

Let us now imagine a cloudy autumn morning, almost dark and completely still: the day after Agnes's death. The layers-out have come—two widows, aged and experienced. Two other women are also there to clean and tidy up. The house is full of whispering voices and the smell of coffee.

The layers-out shut themselves up in the bedroom with the dead woman and perform their important task with ceremonious scrupulousness. They wash, comb, clothe, and make up the body, and fill out the cheeks with cotton wool. The long white stockings, the white satin shoes, the petticoat, and the smooth, newly ironed gown with the wide sleeves. The little bonnet over the hair with its discreet ribbon under the chin. Finally, the yellow rose between the softly colored hands. Then the candles are lighted, the sheets hung in front of the windows, the worldly bed hangings removed, the room cleared of pictures and furniture. The doors into the drawing room are thrown open, and the two layers-out, who have now changed into their formal Sunday best of seemly black silk, stand curtsying with the self-assurance of professional, yet humble pride. They invite the old chaplain and the sisters and the maidservant to enter this room, dedicated by their diligence and worthy knowledge.

> *I don't quite know how to describe this. It should all be like a* movement—*almost a ritual dance without being exaggerated. Perhaps a pavane for a dead infanta.*

The chaplain, who is an old and holy man, turns around to make sure that the old cleaning women are also present in the doorway, that everyone has stopped coughing and scraping their feet, that all is quiet. His face is calm, severely dignified, seemly; his lean body is enclosed in the black uniform of office. When all is quiet he clasps his hands and says a prayer over the dead Agnes.

"God, our Father, in His infinite wisdom and mercy, has decided to call you home in the flower of your youth. Prior to that, He found you worthy to bear a heavy and prolonged suffering. You submitted to it patiently and uncomplainingly, in the certain knowledge that your sins would be forgiven through the death on the Cross of your Lord Jesus Christ. May your Father in Heaven have mercy on your soul when you step into His presence. May He let His angels disrobe you of the memory of your earthly pain."

The chaplain falls silent, as though overcome. He stands perplexed, with his eyes shut. Then he kneels down stiffly; the others present also kneel without understanding, uncertain and unaccustomed. He passes one hand across his eyes and supports himself against a chair with the other.

"If it is so that you have gathered our suffering in your poor body, if it is so that you have borne it with you through death, if it is so that you meet God over there in the other land, if it is so that He turns His face toward you, if it is so that you can then speak the language that this God understands, if it is so that you can then speak to this God. If it so, pray for us. Agnes, my dear little child, listen to what I am now telling you. Pray for us who are left here on the dark, dirty earth under an empty and cruel Heaven. Lay your burden of suffering at God's feet and ask Him to pardon us. Ask Him to free us at last from our anxiety, our weariness, and our deep doubt. Ask Him for a meaning to our lives. Agnes, you who have suffered so unimaginably and so long, *you must be worthy to plead our cause.*"

Bewildered and exhausted, the chaplain gets to his feet and looks about him with an embarrassed and sad smile. He feels there is need of an explanation: "She was my comfirmation child. We often had long and intimate talks. Her faith was stronger than mine."

He breaks off and again becomes the official who knows how to conduct himself in the proper manner. His smile grows formal. He smooths his cassock, which has puckered across his stomach, then moves around and shakes hands with everyone. To Karin: "If you will come to my office tomorrow, we can discuss the formalities of the funeral."

Maria offers to see the old clergyman to the door. When they are by themselves Maria takes him by the arm: "May I have a word with you, Uncle Isak?"

He nods rather vaguely. Maria opens the door of an almost empty room (containing nothing but a large table by the window and an old kitchen chair in the middle of the floor). She goes over to the window and props her arms against the table. The old man remains standing just inside the door. "What do you want to say to me, Maria?"

"Can you, Uncle Isak, forgive me my sins? This moment?"

The old man pauses before answering, then says: "I cannot forgive you anything. But you can forgive yourself."

"Please say a blessing over me," Maria says urgently. "Please, I want you to."

He lays his hand on her shoulder, and she kneels down willingly. Raising her head, she looks up at him trustfully and expectantly. He leans forward and quickly makes the sign of the cross over her brow. She closes her eyes, reveling in it.

"Maria, you who bear the name of the Holy Virgin, may you always live in your own light. Free from guilt and remorse. Enclosed in the purity that is your freedom."

Again making the sign of the cross over her brow, he asks gently: "Are you satisfied now?"

"Yes, I think so," Maria answers.

10.

Let us deal with an episode from Maria's earlier life. The setting is the same, however. I mean the fluid red colors, the heavy furniture, the rich curtains, the pictures, the carpets. (Come to that, everything that happens in our film can easily take place in the same environment; that in itself is no trouble.) The family doctor is on an evening visit. Anna's three-year-old daughter is ill. Anna is sitting on a chair, not weeping, in full control of herself; it is just that her shoulders have become so heavy and round. He finishes his examination and goes out into the kitchen, where he washes his hands in a basin already put out for him. He dries his large, pale hands very carefully and then puts on his jacket, which Maria is holding for him. Turning to Anna, he says something kind and encouraging. She bobs, but says nothing. He pats her cheek; she lowers her head and bobs again.

"I expect you're hungry, Doctor," Maria says. "We've laid the table in the dining room, if you'd care for some supper."

The doctor thanks her politely and accepts with pleasure. The table is laid at one end. They sit down and Maria pours out some wine. They toast each other in silence.

"Agnes and Karin are still in Italy," Maria says, making conversation. "I had a letter from them last week—why no, it was on Wednesday. Agnes is much better. She's not coughing any more and has taken up her painting again. Karin's husband is going down to join them at Easter. They're having good weather—almost summer —though the evenings are chilly, of course."

The doctor lifts his head and regards her without any pretense "Where's your husband?" he asks.

"Joakim's in town on business and won't be back until tomorrow. I told him I was going to ask you to come and look at Anna's little girl. He sent his regards."

The doctor gives a little smile and sips his wine. Maria drains her glass and pours out more wine for herself and the guest.

"I've made up a bed for you in the guest room," Maria says abruptly. "The weather's much too bad for you to go home this evening."

The doctor smiles to himself, and devotes himself for a time to the good food.

"You've changed," Maria declares. "Is there someone else?"

"There's always someone else," the doctor replies gravely. "Anyway, I didn't think that that problem interested you."

"It doesn't, either," Maria answers with a sigh.

The guest room is warm and cozy. A fire glows in the tiled stove;

the large bed with all its pillows and bolsters gleams in the dim light. The doctor has settled down in an easy chair; he has put on his spectacles and is deep in a book. There is a knock at the door. Before he has time to answer, it opens and Maria comes in. She is in her nightgown and peignoir; her long hair hangs loose. The doctor gets up, lets the book fall to the floor, takes her by the arms.

"You have spectacles nowadays," she says.

He gives her a searching look. "What is it you want?" he asks.

"Why are you so formal?" Maria whispers. "Can't we forget the past?" She kisses him lightly on the cheek, then at the corner of the mouth, then on the lips.

The doctor smiles, but it is not a nice smile. Holding her firmly by the arms, he turns her toward the wall mirror. He lifts the table lamp, places it on a small shelf so that it illuminates their faces, and turns up the wick. Maria offers no resistance. She falls in with this trustingly, as if it were an interesting game, something to be taken advantage of in order to make the moment more exciting. She confronts her reflection calmly.

"Take a good look at yourself, Marie!" (He calls her Marie, not Maria.) "You are beautiful. Perhaps more beautiful than before. But you have changed. I want you to see that you've changed. Your eyes nowadays cast quick, calculating side glances. Before, you looked straight ahead, openly, without disguising yourself. Your mouth has taken on an expression of discontent and hunger. It used to be so soft! Your complexion is paler than before; you use makeup. Your fine, broad forehead now has four scratches above each eyebrow— no, you can't see in this light, but it's noticeable in broad daylight. Do you know where those scratches come from? It's indifference that has made its mark there. Do you see this fine line from the ear to the point of the chin? It's no longer so implicit. It shows you're easygoing and indolent. And here at the root of the nose—can you see? You sneer too often, Marie! Why do you sneer? Do you see, Marie? And under your eyes the sharp, almost invisible wrinkles of boredom and impatience."

Maria has listened to the doctor's lecture with a growing smile. "You're scolding me," she says gently. "Can you really see all that in my face?"

"No," the doctor replies. "I feel it when you kiss me."

She shakes her head. "You're just pulling my leg," she says with a laugh, but grows suddenly serious. "I know where you see it," she says quickly.

"And where would that be?"

"You see it in yourself. You see it in yourself."

The doctor gives a slight nod and turns her toward him.

"It's because we're so alike, you and I," she says lightly.

"Alike in what way?" he asks.

"Oh, I can't be bothered figuring it out and I don't care anyway," Maria says.

Then he says suddenly: "Selfishness. Coldness, indifference."

"Your arguments have nearly always bored me," Maria whispers, pouting. "You love saying interesting things. About yourself and other people."

"And you love looking at yourself in the mirror. Is there any difference?" He kisses her and touches her lightly. "Are there no extenuating circumstances for people such as you and I?" he asks suddenly.

"I've no need of being pardoned," Maria replies, kissing him again and again.

Next morning, Joakim, Maria's husband, returns from his business trip. He is a slim, restless person with finely chiseled features and dark, searching eyes. He has withdrawn to his study and immersed himself in the daily paper. Now and then he cautiously sips the coffee that Anna has just served him.

Maria has come into the room and sat down on the broad sofa. She is dandling her small daughter and talking baby talk to her and the child's doll.

"The doctor was here yesterday," Maria says to her husband. "He sent you his regards and hopes you can soon meet and play chess again. I asked him to stay the night—it was such dirty weather last evening. He left early this morning before any of us were up. Did you have a nice time in town or was it nothing but hard work?"

Her husband lowers his paper and nods without saying anything. He sips his coffee and smiles at his daughter, who holds up her doll.

"We've had an invitation from the Egermans at Högsäter," Maria goes on. "They want us to stay over Easter. I think it would be rather nice, I mean, for a change. What do you say? We're supposed to have Aunt Ella here at Easter, of course, but perhaps we can alter that. It's not undiluted joy having Aunt Ella here from morning to night."

"We'll see," Joakim says, folding up the paper very slowly and neatly. Then he finishes his coffee, puts the cup down carefully, leans forward and kisses his daughter on the forehead, and strokes his wife's cheek with the back of his hand. Then he goes into the next room, his bedroom (they sleep in separate rooms).

Maria is suddenly beset by an obscure fear. She walks up and down, biting her hand. She stops and listens. Then she gives up all resistance and hurries into the next room. Her husband is sitting in an uncomfortable armchair, his back to the door. When he hears her footsteps, he tries to turn his head in her direction; his face is pallid and his mouth half open. He has unbuttoned his vest and driven a sharp paper knife between his ribs.

"Help me," he says in a clear, childish voice. The bloodstain spreads on the snow-white shirt.

But Maria takes a few steps backward, until the bookshelf checks her. Then she shakes her head. "No," she says.

He pulls out the knife and throws it on the floor. He begins to cry, sobbing and hiccuping.

From that moment, Maria is haunted by two conflicting yet completely similar mental pictures. One shows her rushing up to her husband and pulling the knife out of his wound, showering him with kisses and protestations, staunching the flow of blood with tender embraces, and pleading for forgiveness. The other picture, which is equally vivid and occurs just as often, shows her forcing the knife deeper into her husband's chest with all her strength, in a moment of stinging satisfaction.

11.

It is the strong, unmoving sunlight which is always most frightening. My cruelest dreams are flooded with unbearable sunlight.

"I want us to be friends," Maria says to Karin. "I want us to touch each other, I want us to talk to each other. After all, we're sisters. We have so many memories in common—we can talk about our childhood! Karin, my dear, it's so strange that we don't touch one another, that we only talk impersonally. Why won't you be my friend? We've been both happy and unhappy, we could go on talking for days and nights on end, we could laugh and cry together, we could hold each other tight. Sometimes as I move about here in the home of our childhood, where everything is both strange and familiar, I feel as if I'm mixed up in a dream and that we're going to be affected by something decisive, something that will change our lives once and for all. I don't know, I don't understand. I'm childish and superficial. You've read so much more than I have, you've thought so much more than I have, and you've much greater experience. Dearest Karin, couldn't we use these days we're together in getting to know one another, in getting close to one another? I can't stand distance and silence. Have I said something to hurt you perhaps? Have I, Karin? It's so easily done, but I swear I didn't mean any harm by it."

The sunlight blazes on the old family portraits. Anna moves silently through the room and leaves the door of the bedroom half open. Agnes can be glimpsed in there, on the white, almost luminous bed. The silence is tangible, can be touched.

Karin shakes her head. "You're wrong," she says with difficulty. "You're wrong. I'm merely afraid."

"What are you afraid of? You're not afraid of me, surely? I don't understand what you mean. Are you afraid to confide in me, don't you trust me? Can't I touch you?"

"No, don't touch me," Karin says. "Don't touch me. I hate any sort of contact. Don't come near me."

Agnes calls to her sisters faintly, her lips move and she calls in a whisper, but they don't hear her.

Anna stops in the doorway and listens. "No, I think it was just a bird outside the window," she says quietly.

Despite Karin's warning, Maria has stood up and she approaches her cautiously with lingering, gentle movements. Then she kneels down in front of her and raises her hand, stroking her over the forehead and cheek. Then she raises the other hand too, and strokes her over the mouth, holds her hands in front of Karin's eyes. Karin sits still and lets it happen.

Now Maria leans toward her and kisses her carefully; first on the cheeks and then on the eyelids, then on the lips. All this is done as a matter of course, without passion but with gentleness.

"No," Karin whispers. "No, I don't want you to do that. I don't want you to."

"Quiet now," Maria whispers, caressing her the whole time quietly and tenderly.

Karin begins to weep. It is not pretty weeping; it is violent, ugly, clumsy, with choking sobs and sudden screams.

"I can't," Karin cries. "I can't. All that which can't be altered. All the guilt. It's constant misery and torment. It's like in hell. I can't breathe any more because of all the guilt."

She regains control of herself and sits with her hands on her knees and her face to the window. (The hard, white light!) Then she suddenly turns to Maria with a polite smile. Her voice is clear and calm. "I'm sorry I lost control of myself," she says. "I don't know what came over me. I suppose it's all the emotion in connection with Agnes's death. We were so fond of her. (*Suddenly she speaks in a different voice.*) Nothing, no one can help me. (*Again she speaks in her usual voice.*) When the funeral is over, I'll ask our solicitor to arrange all the legal formalities. I suppose we'd better sell the house. Before that, we can divide up Agnes's estate—I mean the furniture and other things like china and pictures, the silver and the books. I'm sure we'll come to an agreement. What do you think we should do about Anna? My suggestion is that we each give her a small sum of money, and good riddance to her. We can also give her something that belonged to Agnes. She was so devoted wasn't she? I gather they were quite attached to each other. Now she trails around after us, making herself familiar in the most uncalled-for way. I think that (*with a change of voice*) yes, it's true, I've thought of suicide many times. I have sleeping tablets. It's disgusting, it's degrading, I'm rotten to the core. It's everlastingly the same, it's (*in her normal voice*) nothing. I mean it's not a serious problem. At any rate not for me. I can assure you that Henrik is a reliable solicitor. (*There is no change of voice.*) He has been my lover for five years. Lover indeed. What a silly word. As if our affair had anything to do with love; it's a dirty itch and a few moments' oblivion. It's a certain revenge on Fredrik, he's (*still no change of voice*) an excellent solicitor. I think I said that just now."

Suddenly she opens her mouth and screams like an animal. Then she falls silent and resumes her former expression. Maria has listened to Karin's monologue without any reaction, but with a cold little smile.

"My husband says I'm such a fumbler and he's right," Karin continues. "I'm clumsy. My hands are too big, you see. They won't obey me. Now you're smiling with embarrassment. This wasn't the kind of conversation you had imagined. Do you realize how I hate you? Do you realize how absurd I think you are with your coquettishness and your wet smiles? How have I stood you so long, and never said a word? I know who you are, you with your caresses and your false promises. Can you grasp how anyone can live with so much hate as I have to bear? There is no pity, no relief, no help, nothing. *And I see!* Nothing escapes me. Why can't I stand Anna's imploring eyes, why do I strike her face? Why did I think Agnes was disgusting, with her limpness and her meddlesomeness and her old-maidishness? And her ridiculous artistic ambitions? Now you can hear what it sounds like when Karin talks."

She laughs and gets up. "You smile your cold little smile. What are you thinking? Would you like to tell me? May I hear your opinion? No, just as I thought. You prefer to keep silent. You're right there, Maria! (*Suddenly she speaks in a different voice.*) Perhaps you mean well. Perhaps you just want to get to know your sister. Poor little Maria, how I've frightened you. I'm only talking, don't you see. No, that's not true either. Look me in the eyes. No, look at me, Maria."

As though on a mutual impulse, in a burst of affection, the sisters embrace each other. Their faces are now gentle; they speak quietly and penetratingly.

"Dearest Maria," Karin says, "I hear myself saying all those incredibly horrible words. It's me, yet not me."

"I don't mean to be cold and indifferent," Maria says almost simultaneously. "It's a sort of disease. I want to be warm and kind and tender."

"Can't we make a new start?" Karin says pleadingly. "Can't we wipe out all we've said and done to each other?"

"I think if we helped each other we could change everything," Maria says. "We know each other so well, you see. And we've never used our knowledge except to hurt each other."

They hold each other's hands. They look into each other's eyes and smile at each other, openly, with no guile or anxiety.

12.

Next to the kitchen, I picture a space, a kind of storeroom with laundry baskets full of apples and shelves cluttered with all kinds of household utensils. In the middle of the floor stands a hand mangle. Anna is working alone at the green iron wheel, which she has to exert all her strength to turn. The damp, sweet-smelling towels are pressed slowly through the rollers. Then the wheel stops; she hangs over the handle and the board, getting her breath.

She hears a peculiar sound—very faint, very remote. She lifts her head, straining her ears. No—it can't be heard any more. But while she is busy putting the newly mangled towels in the linen cupboard, she again hears the despairing childish sobs. She listens, turning her head toward the big, empty rooms. Yes, it must be there; it must be someone in need of comfort. She goes through the dining room into the drawing room. There, as in the other rooms, the light is without any shadows, like the light just before sunrise. (Yet, after all, perhaps it is a cloudy afternoon!) Maria is sitting in a chair, petrified, like a wax figure. Karin is standing by the window, staring out into the vague light. Anna tries to speak to them, but her voice is inaudible. She opens her mouth; her lips form the words, she can hear her own breathing, she can also hear the rustle of her skirt, her foot against the carpet, she can hear the unceasing voices of the clocks, but she cannot speak.

Maria turns her head and looks at her with a despairing appeal. Maria moves her mouth, breathes deeply, but what she tries to say is unintelligible. Anna goes over to Karin at the window, and sees that Karin wants to tell her something. Cautiously she touches Karin's eyelids with her fingertips. But it's useless. Karin cannot make herself heard either. Now the child's weeping is heard again, close at hand and unmistakable.

Anna hurries as best she can; every step is leaden, every movement is impossible. She hurries into the bedroom, where Agnes is resting. There is a half light. The two candles by the bed shine with pale, sleepy flames. Sheets in front of the windows. The smell of withering roses. The little mantelpiece clock with the shepherd.

The weeping has stopped.

I don't quite know how to explain this. What is important is that everything in this situation appears natural—real and yet mysterious, in a tension.

Anna now sees that the dead woman has been crying; the tears have run down her cheeks onto the white lace-edged pillowcase. Although the eyes are shut, the eyelids twitch faintly. Anna tries again to speak, but cannot. So she sits down on the edge of the bed, waiting, not anxious or upset. She grasps Agnes's thin hands without disturbing their position. Agnes's lips begin to move and then she speaks in a faraway voice which is changed and laborious, infinitely weary.

"Are you afraid of me now?" she asks.

Anna shakes her head. No, she's not afraid.

"I am dead, you see," Agnes says.

Anna merely looks at Agnes and holds her hands tightly.

"The trouble is I can't get to sleep. I can't leave you all." She moans softly and tears are squeezed out from under the closed eyelids. "Can't anyone help me?" she moans. "I'm so tired."

"It's only a dream," Anna whispers in a flash of inspiration.

"No, it's not a dream," Agnes answers tormentedly. "For you perhaps it's a dream. But not for me."

> How tired I am of hearing that imagination must always be held responsible to the intellect! Inspiration should be well behaved in the face of reality's accusations. Does Agnes perhaps only seem to be dead? Is she a ghost? Are we going to make a ghost film? No, I hadn't thought of making a ghost film. So there should be a meaning. What is it? What is Bergman getting at? Can one concoct just anything? What anything?
>
> These ladies have been my companions for several months; they have presented themselves in situations and scenes which I try to reproduce as well as I can. Death is the extreme of loneliness; that is what is so important. Agnes's death has been caught up halfway out into the void. I can't see that there's anything odd about that. Yes, by Christ there is! This situation has never been known, either in reality or at the movies.
>
> Imagination should be ashamed; it's humiliating, but necessary. Every day I make up my mind that this lawsuit is tiring, unpleasant, and moreover meaningless. Every day I promise myself to lay aside this project of my constant vexation. Every day I retract my decision and start again or tear up what I've written or go on building. The desire is indefinite but persistent. What is it I want with these pictures? What, once again, is the so-called meaning? I don't know, I can never say with any certainty. I might possibly be able to make some suitable rationalizations. All I know is that I am driven by a desire to lay bare a state of affairs, to create a space in the midst of a chaos of confusion and conflicting impulses, a space in which with a joint effort, imagination and the wish for form crystallize a component in my sense of being alive: the unreasonable and never-satisfied longing for fellowship, the clumsy attempts to do away with distance and isolation.

Don't take this as directions for use, or do take it as directions for use, whatever you damn well like, as long as it is used; regard it as a pretext for turning up your nose if necessary. I can't help it if it's like this, even if I think it's peculiar—in some cases (seen with the objective eyes of the intellect) embarrassing. I'm trying to keep to the point; at all events I speak with my own voice and appear in my own expensive suit. Every day I cross off on my desk calendar the distance I have covered. At the moment there is no terminus; this gives me a feeling composed of rage, obstinacy, and self-pity.

However, a person involved in an artistic scuffle never does feel very well; there's nothing very strange in that. Nonetheless, I have this outburst of impatience and boredom. Perhaps it's the day which is dark, rainy, or autumnal. Perhaps it's the desperation of standing at some invisible boundary or beating at it without being able to get past it. Perhaps I hear a yawn from one of my co-workers (the audience can yawn to their hearts' content).

So I repeat: This can't be comprehended by the intellect. It's a matter between the imagination and the feelings. There will be time enough for us to be sensible, deliberate, and wise when we set about the scenic realization of our project, when we materialize all these states of mind, tensions, and movements. While I write and while you read, we must be shamelessly easy to influence—open.

Every new film is an adventure. I think it was Schiller who said that one must compromise oneself in time. I'd like to stretch these words of wisdom and say that one must never stop compromising oneself. End of outburst.

This is the continuation and conclusion of the dream.

Shadowless twilight. The four women's faces, distinct, brought out, clearly defined—eyes, lips, skin. The movements of hands. The bedroom—remote, almost floating; the sick light from the candles by the bed. The pale surfaces; the rectangles of the windows covered with white sheets.

Anna is standing in the doorway between the two rooms. "Karin, Agnes wants you."

Without any visible reaction, her eyes downcast, Karin goes

quickly into the bedroom. She stops at the foot of the bed. In a whisper, Agnes asks her to hold her hands, to warm her, to kiss her. Agnes says that everything around her is emptiness; she begs her sister to help her. Agnes asks Karin to stay with her until the horror has passed.

"I can't," Karin says. "There isn't a soul who'd do what you ask. I'm alive and I don't want anything to do with your death. Perhaps if I loved you. But I don't. What you ask of me is repulsive. I'll leave you now. In a few days, I'm going away."

Agnes listens with her eyes shut.

Karin leaves the bedroom. The clock strikes the hour. The trees are shaken by a gust of wind. Then it is still once more. Anna is standing in the doorway for the second time.

"Maria, Agnes wants you."

Maria makes a gesture of undisguised horror. Then she pulls herself together and casts a quick glance at Karin, whose face is ashen, torn open.

Maria walks toward the bed, but stops. Agnes tells her not to be afraid, asks her to touch her, to speak to her, to hold her hands, to warm her. Faltering, Maria takes the last step. Frightened and hesitating, she takes her sister's hands.

"I'll gladly stay with you as long as you need me," Maria says. "You *are* my sister and I don't want to leave you alone. I feel so terribly sorry for you. Do you remember when we were little and played together in the twilight? Suddenly, and at the same moment, we felt afraid and cuddled together and held each other tight. It's the same now. Isn't it?"

"I can't hear what you're saying," Agnes complains. "You must speak louder and you must lean closer."

Maria leans closer. She shuts her eyes and face, overcome with cold terror and nausea. Agnes lifts her hand with a somnambulistic movement and removes the combs from Maria's hair. It tumbles down over their faces. Then Agnes puts her hand behind Maria's neck and pulls her violently to her, pressing her lips against Maria's mouth.

Maria screams and wrenches herself away, wiping her mouth with her hand; she staggers backward, spits. Then she flees out into the next room, tries to open the doors to the dining room, but they are shut; tries to open the doors to the hall, but they are locked. The clocks strike and the trees in the park are shaken by another gust of wind.

Then Agnes's lament is heard, very faint and far away, but persistent.

Anna is standing in the doorway.

"Agnes wants me to stay with her," she says. "You needn't be afraid any more. I'll look after her."

"I have my daughter to think of," Maria says. "She must realize that. I have my husband who needs me."

"It's revolting," Karin says. "It's disgusting and meaningless. She has already started to decay. She has great spots on her hands."

"I'll go to her," Anna says. "I'll stay with her."

Anna closes the door. Maria and Karin are left in the paralysis of the dream. Agnes's lament can still be heard. The daylight fades against the panes. The trees of the park stand motionless and black. The women's faces can be vaguely seen in the gathering darkness. All colors are obliterated. The red walls become obscure in the indefinite changing light.

Agnes's lament becomes fainter and fainter (a child crying itself to sleep, but still wailing a little). Then there is complete silence. The weeping ceases. There is silence.

The door opens and Anna can be glimpsed. (Her eyes, her mouth, the heavy body, the broad hands.) "She's asleep now," Anna says, passing through the room, opening the doors.

Maria begins to move to and fro across the floor like a startled bird. She grips her right arm with her left hand, trying to move it. "I don't know what's the matter with my hand," she cries. "What's happened to my hand? I can't move it. It's petrified."

"Don't shout," Karin says. "You might wake Agnes and everything would start all over again. I've no intention of losing my reason. Nothing's going to happen to us. Nothing has happened to us. It was only a dream, the whole thing. Do you hear what I say, Maria? The whole thing was only a dream."

13.

I still go on painting, sculpting, writing, playing. In the old days, I used to imagine that my creative efforts brought me into contact with the outside world, that I left my loneliness. Nowadays I know that this isn't so at all. In the end all my so-called artistic expression is only a desperate protest against death. Despite this, I keep on. No one but Anna sees what I achieve. I've no idea whether it's good or bad. Probably bad. After all, I've seen so little of life. I've never bothered to live among people in their reality. Though I wonder whether *their* reality is any more tangible than mine—I mean my illness.

In this connection perhaps I should say something about Agnes's studio. It is a long, rather spacious room, with curtainless windows facing north. In the middle of the floor is the easel, with an unfinished painting. Agnes's painting is generously colorful and somewhat romantic. Her main subject is flowers. At right angles to one of the end walls stands an old-fashioned piano, littered with sheet music. Above it hangs a large and powerful charcoal drawing of Anna. On a table to the right of the door is a jumble of other results of Agnes's unceasing diligence, some of them rather touching: sculptures in clay, mosaic works, ceramics in bright colors, painting gear, oddments of the most varied kinds, piles of drawings and watercolors. Beneath one window Agnes has placed the battered desk from her childhood, cluttered with books, files, and papers. There is a large photograph of her mother as a young woman. An ingen-

*ious music box, full of old hits and dance tunes. Leaning out
from the corner is a large cupboard with glass doors, containing
everything under the sun—books, bottles of wine and glasses, a
group of Chinese clay figures, a few puppets, an old camera,
and so on. On the wall by the door is a picture or notice. It is a
verse surrounded by small watercolors, and the text runs:*

> *Where is the friend whom everywhere I seek,
> When day breaks still greater is my yearning;
> When day is done I have not found him yet,
> Although my heart is burning.*

14.

Together with their husbands the sisters have returned from the funeral. They have sat down in the drawing room and are warming
themselves with a cup of tea and a glass of sherry while waiting for
the carriages that are to take them to the railway station. Anna is
busy packing and carrying suitcases. She passes through the room
now and then, never idle for a moment. It is snowing gently and
persistently.

The conversation flags. There is a cold, slightly contemptuous politeness between the brothers-in-law. The sisters behave warily.

"Well, it was a bearable funeral," Fredrik says. "Nobody wept or
grew hysterical. The music was nice and the chaplain's address
brief."

"By the way! Shouldn't we do something for Anna?" Joakim asks
suddenly.

Fredrik opens his dark eyes wide in a grimace of astonishment.
"Do what? I'm sorry, but I just don't get your meaning."

"Well, she has looked after Agnes for the last twelve years. What about giving her a consideration in cash or suggesting some sort of employment?"

"Out of the question," Fredrik retorts. "She's young and strong and has had a very easy time of it up to now. We've no call to shoulder the responsibility of her future."

"I've promised her she can take a memento with her," Karin says.

"Of her own choosing?"

"Yes, of course. I think she has the right to that."

"How I detest that kind of spontaneity!" Fredrik says. "But you can't go back on it. We'd better speak to her straightaway."

Maria calls Anna, who enters the room with calm indifference. Joakim explains what they have decided. Anna thinks it over for a moment and then says she doesn't want anything. She says it in such a tone that Fredrik feels annoyed. He shrugs. "She's trying to play a beautiful part. Can't we give her anything for that?"

"So you're leaving at the end of the month, Anna?" Karin asks.

Anna nods.

"Then we've nothing more to attend to for the moment," Joakim says, getting up briskly. "We must be going, before the roads to the station are completely snowed up."

They prepare to leave. Karin and Maria shake hands with Anna and thank her for all she has done. Maria presses a banknote into the servant's hand; she accepts it and bobs by way of thanks. Karin waits in the doorway and says she wants a word with Maria. They move back into the drawing room. They are both harassed and uncertain.

"That evening when we came close to each other," Karin says anxiously. "Have you thought of what we talked about then?"

"Of course I've thought of it," Maria replies, with a smile.

"Can't we keep our good resolutions?"

"My dear Karin, why ever shouldn't we?"

"I don't know. It's all so different from that evening."

"I think we've got closer to each other," Maria says, with a smile.

"What are you thinking of?" Karin asks suddenly.

"I'm thinking of what we were talking about," Maria replies, caught out.

"No, you're not," Karin snaps.

"I'm thinking that Joakim is waiting for me, and that's one thing he hates. I can't think why you suddenly call me to account for my thoughts. What are you getting at?"

"Nothing," Karin replies wearily.

"Well, if there's nothing you want I hope you won't be hurt if I say goodbye," Maria says coldly.

"You touched me," Karin says suddenly, looking gravely at her sister. "Don't you remember?"

"I can't possibly remember every silly thing, and above all I *won't* be made to answer for them. Goodbye, Karin dear. Look after yourself and give my love to the children. I expect I'll see you again at Twelfth Night as usual."

She makes to kiss Karin's cheek, but Karin avoids her. Maria smiles apologetically and shakes her head. "What a pity," she says, and walks quickly out of the room.

Everyone has gone.

Now Anna is alone. She moves from room to room, unable to make up her mind to light a lamp or do anything sensible. Instead, she becomes more and more upset. Now and then she presses her hand to her mouth as though to stifle a scream.

"It's nothing," she says to herself. "It doesn't matter. I know it doesn't matter."

She stands by the window, looking out at the park. The snow is falling more heavily now and the wind has come up. The gloom of twilight deepens, but she still doesn't light a lamp. The smell of withering flowers is mixed with that of cigar smoke and strangers. The trestles are still standing in the room, with the black cloth and the tall candles. Anna listens.

Faintly, very far away and scarcely discernible, she hears the child's crying.

15.

AGNES'S DIARY:

A summer's day. It's cool, almost a tang of autumn in the air, yet so nice and soft. My sisters, Karin and Maria, have come to see me. It's wonderful to be together again like in the old days—like in our childhood. I'm feeling much better, too. We can even go for a little walk together—such an event for me, especially as I haven't been out-of-doors for so long. We strolled down to the old swinging seat in the oak tree. Then the four of us (Anna came too) sat in the swing and let it rock to and fro, slowly and gently.

I closed my eyes and felt the breeze and the sun on my face. All my aches and pains were gone. The people I'm most fond of in the world were with me. I could hear them chatting round about me, I felt the presence of their bodies, the warmth of their hands. I closed my eyes tightly, trying to cling to the moment and thinking: Come what may, this is happiness. I can't wish for anything better. Now, for a few minutes, I can experience perfection. And I feel a great gratitude to my life, which gives me so much.

THE HOUR OF THE WOLF

The hour of the wolf is the hour between night and dawn. It is the hour when most people die, when sleep is deepest, when nightmares are most real. It is the hour when the sleepless are haunted by their greatest dread, when ghosts and demons are most powerful. The hour of the wolf is also the hour when most children are born.

Some years ago the painter Johan Borg vanished without a trace from his home on the Frisian island of Baltrum. His wife Alma later gave me Johan's diary, which she had found among his papers. This diary, together with what Alma herself told me, is the basis of this story.

PROLOGUE

Alma hands the coffee cup to the visitor, pushes the sugarbowl across the table, and sits down, heavy and tired. She sits for a while looking at her hands, then raises her eyes and looks at the visitor. She shakes her head.

ALMA No, I don't think I'll go back, why should I? We lived together in this house for nearly seven years. In the winter I can move to the mainland and work in the shop. I've done it other years, when we were short of money. (*She smiles suddenly.*) I don't know much more than what I've told you. And you have the diary. (*Gesture toward the visitor.*) The child is due in a month, the doctor says. He examined me in May, before Johan and I came out here for the last time. It was a Friday when we left; I remember, because I helped Mrs. Broström to arrange goods in the shop and they usually come on Fridays. As soon as we had finished packing we set off. It was rather late in the evening, about ten o'clock I think, but it was still light. We intended staying here until August. We're usually quite alone—he never wanted to meet people, he was afraid of . . . I spoke very little, and he liked that. He liked . . . (*She is silent, and sits looking down. After a while she continues.*)

ALMA We arrived here on the island about three in the morning. The sun had just risen. We fetched a wheelbarrow from a shed down by the beach. Broström, who had brought us over, helped us to drag the baggage up the cliff. (*She is silent.*) When we reached the house, it was a joy to find the apple tree in bloom. (*Pauses.*) Then we noticed footprints in the flowerbed under the kitchen window. Johan was rather annoyed, but we thought nothing more of it until . . . (*Silence.*) No, things were fairly good and we were glad to be home again. Johan was a bit restless, but then he always was when work didn't go well, and it hadn't of late. He slept very badly. And he was afraid—afraid of the dark. It had become much worse during the last few years. (*She is silent, thinking back.*) We led a very regular life. We got up early, I prepared breakfast, then he went off with his work and I tidied up and made lunch, which I took out to him.

ACT ONE

Johan and Alma are standing on the steep, rocky shore. It is midday and there is bright sunlight.

JOHAN   There's something yellow down by the water's edge, see it? I went down to take a closer look, but it was gone. But from up here it looks yellow. I've been working away at that yellow patch for hours. Alma, do you see something yellow? You don't. But without that yellow the canvas is meaningless, and I can't make it fit in. It must be because it was all a mistake from the start, the whole composition. I myself think there's something wrong. Yesterday a goat came along and stood staring at my work. He looked so contemptuous that I lost all desire to work for several hours.

Later that afternoon, by the house. The sunlight is still very strong, almost corrosive.

JOHAN   This old cottage has taken on such a comforting look, don't you think? It's so nice sitting like this with my back against the wall and feeling its warmth through my shirt. Almost like leaning against some big, gentle creature. A mother-animal, Alma. Then in the evening we creep into the mother-animal's belly. I'd like some gooseberry fool one day. Will you make some? Alma, my darling, you really are splendid. Yes, you are. Let me look at you. Stop running back and forth. Heavens, how busy you look! What are you laughing at?

He grabs hold of her and puts his arms around her. At first she resists, but relaxes almost at once and makes herself comfortable.

JOHAN   I know, I'll draw you. I'll draw your neck, your shoulders, and your back. Sit over there. Are you cold? No, I knew it. Do you see that black wall out over the sea? No, don't straighten up. Sit the way you always do. Hold your hair up, will you, so that I see your neck better. Like that. Wait, where are my glasses? Damn, the template is broken again. Soon they won't hold together. Sit still, just like that. If I were to draw you patiently day after day . . .

Inside the cottage. It is the small hours of the night, and there is summer twilight outside the windows. Johan has taken out a sketch-book full of drawings.

JOHAN   What's the time? A quarter past three? Don't fall asleep on me, will you, dear! This is the time when . . . (*Alma yawns.*) Look at this—I haven't shown it to anybody. I have made drawings of them. Come and see. This is the most ordinary specimen: he's practically harmless. I think he's homosexual. Then there's the old lady, the one who's always threatening to take off her hat. Do you know what happens then? Her face comes with it. Here's the worst of them. I call him the bird man. I don't know whether it's a real beak or just a mask. He's incredibly quick, and supposed to be related to Papageno of *The Magic Flute*. Here are the others: the carnivores, the insects, especially the spider men, the schoolmaster with his pointer, and all the chattering women, as hard as nails.

Johan is silent, and sits quite still, staring out the window at the twilight. Alma is almost shivering but doesn't dare to move or speak.

JOHAN   You must keep awake a little longer. In an hour or so it will be light, and then I can sleep. A minute can seem an eternity. It's starting now . . . ten seconds . . . oh, these seconds, how long they are! The minute isn't up yet . . . Now, at last! Now it has gone.

ALMA There's something I've been wondering about for a long time. Are you listening? Well, we've been living together now for seven years. No, that's not what I was going to say. Oh, I know. Isn't it so that old people who have lived together all their lives begin to resemble each other? In the end they have so much in common that not only their thoughts but also their faces take on the same expression. What do you think is the reason? I want us to grow so old that we think each other's thoughts, that we get small, dried-up, wrinkled faces exactly alike. What do you think? Are you asleep?

The next morning. When Alma wakes, Johan has already gone off. She gets up and goes outside to wash. An old lady, wearing a red dress and a large hat which shadows half her face, is standing there. She is leaning on a stick.

THE OLD LADY Don't look so alarmed, my dear. I am not dangerous. Give me your hand. Well? Don't be afraid. Take my hand now. There, at last. Can you feel my hand now? The fingers, the veins under the skin? Are you still afraid of me? Oh well, at my age one's hands do get rather cold. After all, I am two hundred and sixteen. Whatever am I saying, seventy-six, I mean. Well, I must be going. What was I going to say . . . Oh yes, now I remember. In his black satchel, under the bed, is that sketchbook with the drawings you saw last night. He wants to tear them up. Tell him not to. *It would be ill-advised.* And one more thing: in the same satchel he hides his diary. Read it! But don't tell him I said so. He distrusts me. And that is his big failing. Well, don't forget what I have said. No, please don't come with me. It would be too tiring. For me, that is.

Inside the house, Alma finds the diary and begins to read. It begins abruptly on Wednesday, July 22.

> "I have just been ill. Not badly so, but unpleasantly enough. I'm up and about again now (though my legs are rather wobbly) and this morning, punctually as usual, I went to the old seamark down at Kallängen.
>
> "I had been working for an hour or two quite undisturbed when a man came walking along down the beach. He headed straight for me and when he came up he spoke politely."

VON MERKENS   Forgive my intrusion, but for several days I've been considering the best method of approach, and at last I thought the politest thing would be to come straight to the point. First of all, I am an admirer of yours. I venture to say, one of your warmest admirers. My name is von Merkens. Baron von Merkens. As you may know, I own this island and I live in the old castle on the north side. You know it, don't you? Splendid. Would you and your wife care to dine with us? Any day that suits you. It will be very simple, I assure you, but I have a good cellar. And our salmon-fishing is famous, is it not?

"I thanked the baron for his kind invitation. He raised his hat and went back the same way he had come."

Alma turns the pages of the diary and goes on reading:

"Thursday, July 23. A hot, hazy day.
"I looked up from my work. A blond, uncommonly beautiful woman sat facing me.
"She looked at me for a while, then began to unbutton her dress, exposing her left breast."

VERONICA   Do you see this mark? You must be more careful, my darling, else it will end in disaster. Don't you remember? I was going to a party and had on my green brocade dress. And afterward I had such trouble doing my hair again. And I forgot my gloves.

JOHAN   Your gloves. Wait a moment. I put them in the pocket of my overcoat. I think they're still there.

VERONICA   I've received a letter that I must show you. It was sent yesterday. "You can't see us, but we see you. Horrible things can happen. Dreams can be made known, the end is near. The springs will dry up and other fluids will moisten your white thighs. So it has been decided." I felt quite ill when I read it. How hot your hands are. Have you a temperature? Always when I'm going to see you I get so worked up, isn't it funny? I go about in a dream all afternoon, everything I do is unreal and meaningless. Help me with my zipper, lamb. It always gets caught.

"We made love avidly, impatiently. Then we lay side by side in silence, our thoughts far away. I dozed off."
"When I waked, she was gone. I dressed and set off for

home. The path leads through thickets and a low-growing wood, which draws its nourishment from the sand and crouches before the sea winds. The trees are barely as tall as a man and wretchedly stunted. The afternoon sunlight flashed in my eyes and there was a roar from the sea. Birds wheeled screeching above their nests. Turning around, I saw that someone was following me—a tall lean man in a shabby, old-fashioned trenchcoat. I stopped to let him pass. But he stood still, facing me."

HEERBRAND   What a gale! But it's magnificent, isn't it? This must be an ideal place for a painter. You have lived here for some time. One returns to the scene of the crime, so to speak, and commits new crimes. You look tired. Don't overdo things. I mean, at our age a certain caution is advisable. Young people are tougher. Oh, I know what I'm talking about. My name's Heerbrand, the curator. I finger souls and turn them inside out. And what do I see? I need hardly tell you. I mean, you're an artist. You know the human heart. Who has not seen your facial studies, to say nothing of the self-portraits. Why do you look at me like that? Are you angry? Are your nerves in a bad way? Is something worrying you? You look quite ill, in fact.

"I turned and struck the man. He raised his arms above his head to ward off the blow."

HEERBRAND   Have I said something to offend you? If so, I apologize. Now look, my nose is bleeding. What a nuisance. No, no, don't bother about me, it will soon stop. I'll stay here for a while, lie down in the sand with my head back, and the bleeding will stop. Leave me, that's a good fellow. I beg you. I don't blame you. You really needn't have a bad conscience because of *me*.

"I could still feel the blow in my right hand when I got home. Alma was outside hanging up the wash. She came toward me with a smile and put her arms around my neck and kissed me. I broke away and went inside. I lay on the bed and turned my face to the wall."

Alma shuts the diary and sits for a long time huddled up. She hears Johan coming and is frightened. She hides the diary.

Later in the house; rain is streaming down the windowpanes. During dinner, Alma takes out the account book.

ALMA   I think you'll have to give me some money. What I got at
the beginning of the month is nearly gone and I must pay the
grocer's bill next time we go over to the mainland. It comes to
$38.50. And then there's the milk. No, don't just fork out money
like that. You must take a proper look at my accounts so that you see
I don't steal anything. Come and look now, it's important. At any
rate to me. It won't take long. I got $110 on the third, didn't I?
Then you gave me that rug. It was rather expensive and cost $7.70,
but it's lovely and warm when I have to lie in my own bed! Then
there was the previous bill at the shop, it was a big one as we had to
buy flour and sugar and canned things when we moved out here last
month, it came to over $44—$48.18 to be exact. Then there's the
milk. And pocket money and stamps and the chain for my cycle and
new batteries for the radio and the potato peeler, and soap and deter-
gent and a nailbrush. By the way, you must buy yourself a new
toothbrush! The one you have looks awful. Then there was $11 for
your boy's birthday and a stamp for 18¢. That makes $110 except
for $1.62. Will you add it up and see that it's correct?

*Johan and Alma arrive at the castle for dinner. The other guests are
already sitting on the terrace facing the sea. Von Merkens greets
Alma and Johan with a cordial smile.*

VON MERKENS   Ah, here come our guests of honor. May I introduce
my wife Corinne.

*Baroness von Merkens extends a slender, rather moist hand. She is
very slim and her daringly low-cut black dress exposes her emaciated
shoulders and a yellowish suntan as dry as parchment. Her face,
with large, extraordinary eyes, is thin and scraggy. Her mouth is
large and heavily made up. Her dark hair is combed back in the latest fashion. Her beauty is unusual and rather frightening.*

VON MERKENS   And this is my mother.

*Von Merkens's mother bears traces of vanished beauty but resembles
most of all an old parrot, with beady black eyes and a sharp, prominent nose. Her mouth is incredibly arrogant and she is wearing a
short dinner dress of thick flame-red silk. Heavy jewelry hangs from
her neck and wrists; one wonders whether it is real or not.*

VON MERKENS   My brother Ernst.

Ernst has a tormented face, pallid and embedded in fat. Out of eyes that are screwed up to mere slits peers a soul terrified to the point of madness. His thin fair hair is fluffed up in a cloud above his broad, shiny forehead. Ernst von Merkens is obviously drunk.

VON MERKENS This is Mr. Lindhorst.

Lindhorst, a keeper of archives, extends a large, hard hand, the back of which is completely covered with hair. His flat, sunburned face with bloated cheeks is that of an aged youth. His thick, dark hair has a side parting. He bares his white teeth in a smile and declares warmly that he is one of the artist's most passionate admirers.

VON MERKENS And finally, may I introduce Mr. Heerbrand.

The curator shakes hands and smiles effusively. His large melancholy eyes show no trace of irony or hint of earlier events.

   When the guests have emptied their glasses, Corinne von Merkens suggests that they should go in to dinner. The table is laid in the green drawing room—an almost circular tower room with green silk and a series of valuable engravings on the walls and Empire furniture. On the table stand a pair of heavy Russian silver candelabra. But the carpet under the table is threadbare, there are large patches of damp in the ceiling, and the curtains look faded and dusty. Some of the wineglasses are chipped.

   Johan is placed on the hostess' left. Lindhorst escorts Alma, and the host his mother. Heerbrand sits next to Ernst von Merkens. A fat and incredibly clumsy servant girl, wheezing asthmatically, moves around the table with the soup tureen. As soon as she has clumped out of the room, Ernst von Merkens begins lamenting in a shrill voice.

ERNST Damned awful servant. She's cheap, of course, and my brother can't afford a better one. But it's not his fault all the same. I beg you to note that the reason your soup was so badly served is that I . . . that I . . .

CORINNE We've settled down now. We used to travel a lot. Do you like traveling? I love it. There's nothing as stimulating.

LINDHORST Alma is an ususual and pretty name.

HEERBRAND . . . in this closed circle. Incapable of feeling aggression. A certain bureaucratic desire for revenge. (*Laughs.*)

VON MERKENS . . . humiliations! The pleasure of being humiliated. We still have our fangs intact.

CORINNE Artists must! Oh yes, I'm convinced that you live at least two lives.

ERNST When you and my brother questioned me down at Bloomsfield.

THE MOTHER Nowadays I like to be . . . (*Whispers to Heerbrand, who chokes with laughter.*)

VON MERKENS I bought a picture from a well-known artist. In those days! No comments, my dear Ernst! Then I hung it upside down in my drawing room, and invited the artist together with a lot of nice people who appreciated a good joke.

CORINNE What would *you* say? I'm told you're so touchy.

VON MERKENS How we laughed! Heavens, how we laughed!

ERNST Compassion? Mercy? Understanding? Forgiveness? Thoughtfulness? Of course! It is all said to exist, in large doses and even in the most unexpected quarters.

MOTHER I went all the way down the street, Mr. Heerbrand. It cost me a small fortune. But I wanted to see how much I could stand before . . . (*Whispers.*)

LINDHORST The sores never heal. The pus keeps oozing out. The invection is chronic. Then it's not long till the end. It depends on how strong the heart is.

CORINNE I'm constantly losing weight. I go all over the world consulting specialists. Sometimes it stops, and I even put on a little. But then it starts again. My husband says it's mental and that it began when we lost our money.

ERNST When *I* embezzled the family money. *I* am the culprit, do you hear? *My dishonesty.* Why is Lindhorst sitting here at our table? Why can't we sell out and go away? My fault, my fault! All this suffering! My fault.

MOTHER (*to Heerbrand*) . . . and then, then I wrote: to the devil with your medicines! It's no better, it will never be better. You must operate and cut it away. I'm an old crone. There's a limit, after all. Then he grinned, that professor, and said: "No, baroness, *I* have never heard of any limit."

CORINNE Yes, I have children. Two boys. No, not here. Oh no! They live with their uncle. By the way, I think they are friends of yours. You know Veronica Vogler, don't you? Very well, I am told.

LINDHORST (*laughing*) Why, your hand is shaking!

CORINNE A very beautiful woman.

VON MERKENS What hatred in those eyes.

ERNST Untold sacrifice.

They are all talking at the same time. Presently they rise from the table and go into the big dark library, where a fire is burning in the open fireplace. Von Merkens takes Johan under the arm as though to steady him. Seeing Alma's face, questioning, anxious, he goes and sits beside her and takes her hand.

Lindhorst then presents a puppet show—a scene from The Magic Flute. *The puppet theater is in a corner of the library and the scene is acted behind the proscenium by real singers moving like mario-nettes worked by Lindhorst's practiced hand. When the curtain has been lowered, the guests applaud. Lindhorst steps forward, illumi-nated by the mysteriously glowing footlights of the little theater.*

LINDHORST *The Magic Flute* is the great example. I shall prove it to you. The Speaker has just left Tamino in the dark grove outside the Temple of Wisdom and the youth cries out in the depths of de-spair: "O ew'ge Nacht! wann wirst du schwinden? Wann wird das Licht mein Auge finden?" Mozart, seriously ill, feels these words with a secret intensity. And the chorus and orchestra answer with: "Bald, bald, Jüngling, oder nie!"

Lindhorst picks up one of the small puppets and inspects it. He smiles.

LINDHORST The loveliest, most disturbing music ever written! Tamino asks: "Lebt denn Pamina noch?" He dreams of love as something perfect. The invisible chorus replies: "Pamina lebet noch." Listen to the strange, illogical, but brilliant division: Pa-mi-na, Pa-mi-na. It's no longer the name of a young woman, it's a for-mula, an incantation. Then the ascent out of fear. Tamino is hope-ful: "Sie lebt? Ich danke euch dafür!" With these phrases as a basis, Mozart, in fifty bars, has written his credo. So utterly naked, so deeply, impenetrably personal, and yet quite natural and unforced. A simple fairy tale (Herr Mozart's new machine comedy, as the crit-ics called the piece). A naïve text, in short a commissioned work and yet the highest manifestation of art! Don't you agree, sir, as an artist?

Turning to Johan, Lindhorst awaits his answer. There is sudden si-lence in the darkening room. Faces, eyes, mouths, teeth.

JOHAN   I call myself an artist for want of a better name. In my cre-ative work there is nothing implicit except compulsion. Through no fault of mine I've been pointed out as something extraordinary, a calf with five legs, a freak. I have never fought to attain that position and I shall not fight to keep it. Oh yes, I have felt megalomania waft about my brow, but I think I'm immune. I have only to think for a moment of the unimportance of art in the world of men to cool off. But the compulsion is still there all the same. Perhaps it is a disease or a mania.

CORINNE (*applauding*)   There speaks an artist!

ERNST (*noisily*)   Quite a confession.

VON MERKENS   What courage! What perspicacity!

MOTHER   Wait! I shall give him the rose of victory.

LINDHORST   Let us drink to our artist. He is not only a genius, he is a thinker too. The devil take me, I had no idea.

MOTHER   A glowing rose in your hair!

Mother fumbles in front of Johan's face. The rose with its thorns jerks past his eyes and the old woman's heavy scent clings to him.

MOTHER   Oh! I caught my nail in your cheek. Let me see. Why, it's bleeding. Here's my handkerchief. No, it's clean. To think I could be so clumsy!

CORINNE   Our artist is hurt.

Everyone laughs. Johan joins in as he tries to get a firm hold on old Baroness von Merkens's skinny, waving arms. Suddenly Alma goes up to him, pushing the other woman aside and gripping his shoulders.

ALMA You must calm down. You've drunk too much. Come to me for a while. (*To the others.*) He sleeps badly at nights and that's why drink goes to his head. We'll just get a breath of air on the terrace.

Outside in the moonlight it is cold and still. Mist lies like wet sheets over the lawn. They sit on a bench, Alma holding his hand. The giddiness is going away. The chill night air makes him shiver. He takes repeated deep breaths. Alma sits close beside him with her head bent.

JOHAN Alma, how nicely she had done her hair for the dinner party. She was so scrubbed and neat. She must have been looking forward to it and imagined goodness knows what. What was she thinking now? The dry hand with the strong fingers, the brown cheek, the fine wrinkles at her eyes, the delicate network of veins at her temple. A sad and anxious heart? Wordless affinity? At this moment I'm trying to reach her, a short second of nearness. Does she feel my longing? Is she indifferent to it, since her own feeling is so great that it fills her need to the brim? To reach another human being, to understand him, to know him with all his thousands and thousands of changing moods, not acting parts in a tragic farce but living together in a shared reality. Not words like "captive," "prison," "torture," "jailer," "walls," "shut in," "distance," "void," "dread," and "ghost." Not words like "sentence," "punishment," "forgiveness," "guilty," "erring," "blame," "disgrace," and "sin." No "penalties," "hangmen," or "saints." No "confessions," "nightmares," and "revenge." What gave birth to the thought of a just and vindictive god, prayer's shout of anguish, faith's terrified vigilance or blind fury? Out of what horror of decay rose this monster called the forgiveness of sins, the resurrection of the dead, and life everlasting?

ALMA Oh my dear one . . . I think that . . . if you were to . . . I think that . . . (*Falls silent.*)

Johan looks at her. Suddenly they are surrounded by the others, who have crept up silently, unnoticed.

VON MERKENS (*amiably*) We were getting worried that something had happened.

CORINNE Or that you had gone away.

LINDHORST (*kindly*) I'm most remorseful. Mr. Heerbrand pointed out that my speech about *The Magic Flute* could easily be misconstrued.

MOTHER As a penance I have cut both my nail and the rose's thorns. Look! Put it at your ear and be proud of your genius!

HEERBRAND Alas, yes. We were both sorry and distressed. Artists are artists and philistines are philistines.

VON MERKENS What moonlight, my friends! Let us take a walk in the park.

They stroll through the park in the damp moonlight.

CORINNE We got rather worked up. No wonder, really, we live so much to ourselves. We lost our balance and frightened you, in fact. But you won't desert us now, will you?

VON MERKENS Look, Corinne! At night and by moonlight our castle doesn't look at all bad.

MOTHER Oh, my garter! Turn away, Mr. Heerbrand. Let us talk of the moon!

HEERBRAND (*shouting*) Look at our shadows! What has become of Ernst? Ernst, my dear fellow. Where are you?

ERNST Did someone call? I took another path. I'm ashamed that the park has been so neglected. Think back ten years. It was a showplace for tourists.

They stand at the balustrade by the sea.

VON MERKENS My grandfather had this balustrade built. People used to fall over it a little too often when there were big festivities.

HEERBRAND And it's a sheer drop. Sixty feet?

ERNST Three hundred.

CORINNE Can you feel how it draws you? The whole expanse of sea.

MOTHER   What a roar when the huge breakers . . .

VON MERKENS   The horror of my childhood. Lindhorst! Are you crazy! Get down off the balustrade at once.

LINDHORST (*balancing*)   "The moon goes behind a cloud and it is dark. A violent gust of wind across the sea, a scream, a body spins in the air. Lindhorst is dashed against the jagged rocks. Was it murder, suicide, or an accident? No one knows. Yet another gory secret is added to the gloomy chronicle of the old castle."

VON MERKENS (*hiding his face in his hands*)   Oh, God!

LINDHORST   I am forty-six. Life blazes around me in all its exuberance, but I rush deeper and deeper into the labyrinth. (*Laughs.*) What nonsense! Redemption through a woman. So original. And so plausible.

CORINNE   Good. Excellent. You are magnificent. We are full of admiration and you have given us an experience. Come here and I'll give you a kiss.

LINDHORST   At once. (*Kisses her.*) Your lips are ice-cold.

MOTHER (*laughing*)   That too!

They walk deeper into the park. Alma comes close to Johan and cautiously puts her arm around his waist.

ALMA (*whispering*)   We never kiss each other, have you thought of that? I can almost count our kisses.

HEERBRAND   There's something that scares me out of my wits. I meet a strange man on the road. We talk of this and that. Suddenly he turns and strikes me on the cheek. His face is deathly pale and his eyes blaze with hatred. I am quite at a loss. I feel sick and my nose starts to bleed. I stand there stammering out a few incoherent excuses. Horribly upset. And I ask myself when the man has disappeared: "Is it true? Must it be like that?"

Heerbrand's voice grows shrill. He turns around appealingly toward the moonlit faces. They return to the castle. Dawn is breaking; the clock in the tower strikes three.

CORINNE (*to Johan*)   Are you going already? No, no! Before you go you must see where I've hung your picture. Alma, my dear, come with us. Oh, she's asleep. We won't disturb her.

ALMA   No, I'm not asleep.

They go to the bedroom.

CORINNE   Come, both of you. It won't take long. Just look at the view! The sun will rise soon. Do come in. I have furnished my bedroom entirely to my own taste. How do you like it? Here's the picture. Facing my bed. I can see it every morning and evening. It has become part of my lonely life.

On the wall opposite the bed is Johan's portrait of Veronica—the calm, pale face, and the dark, wide-open eyes.

CORINNE   I love her. How long did you live together? Forgive such a personal question.

ALMA   Thirteen years.

CORINNE   Oh, he has told you. He loved her, didn't he? I need not ask. It was a big scandal at the time. But *so* romantic. We all envied poor Veronica Vogler.

ALMA   Oh!

CORINNE   Jealous?

ALMA   No, I don't think so.

CORINNE   My husband is rather jealous. He is a splendid lover. Look at this mark, by the way. It's a scar from another man's, shall we say, advances. A perpetual source of renewed excitement. It's all very trivial, of course, but to me it is stimulating. But soon I'll have to think up something new. This mark can't keep its fascination forever. (*Laughs.*) Can you help me? Alma, my dear, don't be cross with me, I was only joking. A silly joke, wasn't it? Let us go down to the others.

Corinne straightens her stocking, pulls her skirt down, and combs her hair. She gives a friendly laugh.

CORINNE   Anyway, I have bought myself a fairly large slice of your husband. (*Pointing to the picture.*) Haven't I?

In the library there is a great commotion, with everyone running about calling Ernst. Baron von Merkens hands his wife a note and hurries out onto the terrace.

CORINNE   Please help me read it, I haven't my glasses.

Johan goes over to the window, where the dawn light is gray and heavy with rain, and reads the following:

JOHAN   "I have never received any punishment, only forgiveness. I don't wish to be ungrateful, but you have done me a big injustice. Every man must bear his punishment, otherwise he can't go on."

CORINNE   On our walk? Yes, he was with us but suddenly disappeared. I know. He had a clothesline in his hand. Then he disappeared and came back and didn't have . . .

After a few minutes' search in the park they find Ernst von Merkens. He has hanged himself.

Alma and Johan are on their way home. It is drizzling and the sea breaks in white foam down on the sandbanks. Suddenly she stops, standing with clenched hands and looking at her husband with a mute, almost insane, despair. He goes up to her, but she shakes her head and shuts her eyes.

ALMA   I want to tell you that I've read your diary and I'm nearly ill with fear. No, wait. Let me finish. I want to say something I've been thinking about the last few days. This is what I've thought: I can see that something is happening the whole time. Something terrible, just because it can't be called anything. But don't think I'm going to run away from you—no, I'm not going to run away, however frightened I am. One thing more: they want to part us. They want you to themselves. If I'm with you it will be much harder. Johan, they can't make me run away from you however hard they try. I'm staying. I'm staying as long as . . .

She begins to weep. Johan tries to touch her, but she draws away. He realizes in a flash that her grief applies only to herself. For the first time she is leaving him outside.

ACT TWO

Alma and Johan are at their house. It is one of those rare, impenetrably dark nights when the sea is quiet. They have already stayed awake for several hours. Alma is very tired.

JOHAN There was a time when the nights were for sleep, a deep, dreamless sleep. "The death of each day's life . . . great nature's second course, chief nourisher in life's feast." Shakespeare. To sleep. To wake unafraid.

ALMA Yes.

JOHAN Are you tired?

ALMA Not so very.

JOHAN We've stayed up every night now until dawn. But this hour is the worst. Do you know what it's called?

Alma shakes her head.

JOHAN The old folk called it the hour of the wolf. It's the hour when most people die. It's the hour when most children are born. Now is when nightmares come to us. And if we are awake . . .

ALMA . . . we are afraid.

JOHAN We are afraid. (*He holds his hands in front of his face.*) Oh, my dear!

ALMA What?

JOHAN No, it's nothing. It just made me think of something. From my childhood.

ALMA The batteries in the radio are dead.

JOHAN Would you like to hear?

Alma nods.

JOHAN I suddenly thought of it. The dark wardrobe. It was a kind of punishment. They pushed me into the wardrobe and shut the door. There wasn't a sound, and it was pitch-dark. I was mad with fear and I pounded and kicked. You see, they had told me that a little man lived in that wardrobe—a cross between a troll and a brownie. He could gnaw the toes off naughty children. When I stopped kicking I suddenly heard something rustling in a corner. I knew that my hour had come. In silent panic I started climbing on shoe boxes and shelves, I tried to heave myself up, clothes fell down all around me, I lost my grip and fell, striking out wildly to save myself from that little creature. Howling with terror, I asked to be forgiven. My capitulation was heard. The door was opened and I could step out into the daylight.

My father said: "Mother tells me that you are sorry." "Yes," I answered. "Please, please forgive me." "Then get ready on the green sofa," he said. I went over to the green sofa in Father's study and put a couple of cushions one on top of the other. Then I went and got the cane, took down my pants and bent down over the green cushions. "How many strokes do you deserve?" my father asked. "As many as possible," I replied. Then he caned me. Hard, but not unbearably. When the punishment was over I pulled my pants up and took the cane back to the corner behind the bookshelf. Then I turned to Mother and said: "Do you forgive me now, Mother?" "Of course I forgive you," she replied, putting out her hand, which I kissed. Then I turned to my father. "Do you forgive me now, Father?" "Now I forgive you," he replied. He too put out his hand and I kissed it. (*He is silent.*) Alma, are you listening?

ALMA   Yes. I've been listening all the time. I haven't been asleep. I'm not even tired any more. (*Pause.*)

JOHAN (*looking at her*)   Then I'll tell you something else. (*Pause.*) Another boy and I used to play in a hospital park. The place that attracted us most was a small brick building with a black roof and windows of frosted glass. It was where they kept people who had just died. One Sunday afternoon, with the snow thawing in the spring sun, we got into the mortuary. In the little chapel there was a coffin which was already sealed up and almost covered with flowers. The other room was bigger. Several bodies were lying there under white sheets. The sun was shining brightly on the blind windows, but in here it was cold, like in a cellar, and there was a musty, sickly smell. Suddenly I heard a door closing. It was my friend sneaking off. I was alone with the dead. Frightened but fascinated, I went from one to the other, lifting a corner of the sheet and studying their features. They looked artificial more than anything else. One of them was a woman with red hair, a pretty little turned-up nose, and gold rings in her well-shaped ears. Her large mouth was bluish-white, her lips were slightly parted, revealing a row of even white teeth. I drew the sheet off her. She had a heavy, voluptuous body and big thighs.

I gazed at the dead woman for a long time, bewitched. Then I raised my hand and touched her face, her ears, her shoulders, her breasts. I let my fingertips glide over the curve of her hips, the auburn tuft of hair covering the genitals, her long thick thighs.

JOHAN   It was my first experience of a naked woman. (*He is silent.*) Alma, Alma, are you listening or are you asleep?

ALMA   No, I'm awake. My back is aching. Not the faintest sign of dawn yet. How quiet it is. It's strange when the sea is so still for once. Horrid in some way. Don't you think?

JOHAN   Why are you crying?

ALMA   I'm not crying. I was just thinking of the child. And this great, silent darkness. It's as if it would never be light again.

JOHAN   Poor you.

ALMA   Take my hand. There, that's better.

JOHAN I'll tell you something strange. Something horrible, Alma. It happened a few weeks ago.

ALMA (*anxiously*) Something horrible?

JOHAN Do you remember the day I came home and said I'd been bitten by a snake?

ALMA Yes.

JOHAN It was no snakebite.

ALMA What was it then?

JOHAN If I tell you, promise never to . . . I didn't think I'd ever tell anyone. I don't even know if . . .

ALMA (*frightened*) You *must* tell me.

JOHAN You must never let anyone know.

ALMA I promise. I will never let anyone know.

JOHAN You remember that place with the big slabs of rock and that sheer drop where the water's deep? We were there once or twice at the beginning of the summer. I used to have it to myself. Remember?

Alma nods. She is numb with tiredness.

JOHAN It was a hot day—sultry but no sun. I hadn't had much luck with my fishing but I'd caught enough not to give up. Suddenly I noticed that I was not alone. A scrawny little boy in tattered jeans and a faded striped shirt was watching me a few yards away. He was barefooted and his arms were folded. His face was very thin and narrow, the eyes were light and quite expressionless, his hair almost white. His nose was short and flat. His mouth and jaws, on the other hand, were remarkably well developed.

After staring at me for a few minutes he moved to where I couldn't see him without turning around. I then found that he was standing just behind me. I had a nasty feeling that he wanted to push me into the water. Suddenly he ran silently up the smooth, sloping rock and stood looking at my painting on the easel. I began to seethe with rage. Rage and a feeling I can't explain—rather like when a strange, treacherous-looking dog runs up to you. He left my picture and bounded just as silently down to the spot where I had laid my catch. He counted the fish and grinned to himself.

I tired of this peculiar game and began gathering up my things. He had lain down on his back with his arms under his neck and one leg over the other. I looked around for my clothes and put on my shirt and pants. My wristwatch had been in a shoe and when I went to put it on I found it was gone. I turned to the boy and asked if he had taken it. He lay there without moving. I went up and, standing over him, repeated my question. He didn't move. But the smile vanished from his thin lips and his nose went white.

I bent down quickly and grabbed him by the scruff of the neck to lift him off the ground. He clung to me and I overbalanced. I saw two cold, pale eyes and open jaws which snapped at my neck. I fought to get free, but the sinewy arms and legs were very strong.

We tumbled over and again he snapped at my neck or shoulder. I flung myself as hard as I could against a rock. The scrawny body seemed to break apart; it released its hold and lay thrashing about and twitching on the rock. It was like an attack of epilepsy—the muscles contracted in almost rhythmical convulsions and the chin was jammed against the chest. I stood there shaking with disgust, staring at the crawling, panting creature.

I went nearer without thinking what I was doing. In a flash he buried his teeth in my bare foot. It hurt like hell, and, reaching for a big stone, I struck at him blindly, over and over again, until he was quite, quite still, until there wasn't a sound.

I rolled the body to the edge and it fell into the deep, black water, vanishing quickly legs first. I could see it sinking toward the darkness, waving, turning over.

There wasn't much blood. I washed it off the slab of rock. My hands also had blood on them and I rinsed them in the icy water. My foot ached and there was an ugly mark, but the wound was not very big and not at all deep. I bandaged it up with my handkerchief and pulled my sock over it.

I sat for several hours looking out over the sea, which changed from gray to yellow without the leaden, sultry sky clearing. At last I got up and limped home.

At one time there was a gray discipline, a strict self-control, a hard daily battle—I remember it all as one remembers a far-off dream. The frontiers are crossed, the other world has broken in over me and

I feel at home in a twilight land. More often than not with fear. Sometimes with relief. An astutely organized everyday life, with the black waters of the other world flowing through it. To tell the truth, there's still a voice which calls for help, an anxious soul which clings to familiar habits, a childish sorrow, an orderly little person's hope of being accepted in spite of everything, a somnolent man's struggle to wake up. All the same, I am convinced deep down that pardon doesn't exist, that the laws are logical, that the course of events blindly follows the beaten track.

There is a tap at the door. The lamp has gone out. Alma and Johan are sitting at the big table, gazing at the grayish rectangle of light from the window.

JOHAN (*frightened*)   Have you locked the door properly?

ALMA (*frightened*)   Yes. I tried it twice to make sure.

The quick tapping is repeated. Then the handle moves down and the door opens slowly with a creak. Mr. Heerbrand, in raincoat and muddy boots, enters, hat in hand.

HEERBRAND   Good morning! I'm so sorry to disturb you. Please forgive me. It looks like a storm. I thought I'd just drop in. I also have a message. May I sit down? I shan't be long-winded. No, thanks, I've given up smoking. There's an invitation from the castle. We're giving a little party. Nothing special. It's just to amuse those poor people. There they are all the year round, getting on each other's nerves. As I said, only a few guests, but I think they will interest you. Veronica Vogler will be there. You'll come, won't you? (*Pause.*) Oh, by the way. A day or two ago von Merkens and I were discussing your chances of defending yourself. I mean, against all the small game on the island. Von Merkens suggested that he should lend you a rifle. I thought it better with a revolver. Well, that's all for this time. Good morning, my friends! I hope to see you at our little party.

Heerbrand vanishes, smiling. The revolver is lying on the table. Alma locks the door, making sure that it really is locked.

ALMA   Is it loaded?

JOHAN   Yes, I think so.

ALMA   Can't we hide it away?

JOHAN   Let's play cards. No? What shall we do then? What do you suggest?

ALMA   You can tell me about Veronica.

JOHAN   What do you want me to tell? It lasted for four years. Well, you know that. We were caught. It was a huge scandal, then it was hushed up. And that was the end of that.

ALMA   That's not what it says in your diary. Shall I read it out to you?

"My obsession with Veronica became at last a torment to us both. I shadowed her in the street and spied on her jealously. I think my passion stimulated her. But she was always passive, vaguely avoiding me. Once or twice it came to frightening scenes utterly devoid of reason. We separated, horrified at what we had done to each other. Then we broke our agreements and started all over again. I became like a dog on a leash. An endless series of humiliations. At last I took to my heels.

"She sought me out, developing a sudden ingenuity and a ruthless energy in tracing my hiding-place. We moved from town to town in an effort to escape her relations and lawyers. Then we got stranded in a back-street hotel in Grenoble when the summer was at its hottest, in a dingy room over a garage. Our nerves were frayed, we were ill and penniless, we tore each other to pieces with abuse and accusations. At the same time there were our embraces, the humiliating lust, the hours of dead sleep. Our mouths met in one long howl. Our bodies dissolved in a sluggish mess of skin and limbs, we carried out in truth the Bible's words that man and woman 'shall be one flesh.' Then her husband came and took her away. I was shut up in a hospital and we didn't see each other for several years." (*Finishes reading.*)

You once said that what you liked about me was that God had made me all in one piece. That I had whole feelings and whole thoughts. You said it was important that such people existed, that most people are split or broken up into small bits. That there are so many invalids. It all sounded so nice. I was flattered and happy and thought I could help you. But I was wrong. I don't understand. I just don't understand. I can't make you out. I'm only afraid.

JOHAN   Go away then. While there's time.

ALMA   I can't do that either. Since I love you.

JOHAN   Love?

ALMA   It's hard to put it any other way. Do you think I want to stay here and perhaps be done to death? Do you think I want to watch you running after that woman? To talk to your phantoms, to guard myself the whole time? Do you think I like it? But I'm still here.

JOHAN   Yes, you're still here.

ALMA   I'm here to stop you. You're not to go to that party. And Veronica can . . . can wait in vain. And you're to get away from this island.

JOHAN   So now I know how it's to be.

ALMA   It must be the way *I* want it to be.

JOHAN   Then we'll say no more about it.

ALMA   No.

JOHAN   Then I can go now?

ALMA   Yes. You can go now.

JOHAN   And you're not going to stop me?

ALMA   I can't stop you.

JOHAN   Yes, you can.

ALMA   No, no, no! I have nothing to do with you.

JOHAN   If *you* go.

ALMA   No, I'll stay here. I shan't look at you. I promise you can go. And when you come back I'll have gone. And you need never . . .

JOHAN   Never?

ALMA   Is there nothing . . . nothing that . . .

JOHAN   I call an obstacle an obstacle.

ALMA   Now you're speaking with a strange voice again.

JOHAN   Give me the book with the drawings. First I'll tear it up. Then I'll be torn up.

ALMA   She warned me against tearing them up.

JOHAN   It's not spite. Don't think it's spite. But now up you get from the table. Now go to the door. Now go out of the door. Now go down the steps. It's not dark any more. You can see your way.

Alma gets up and goes to the door. The revolver is lying on the table.

   In the castle all is silent and still. There is not a soul to be seen. Johan goes from room to room. Windows are open, kerosene lamps are burning, and in one room a little dog comes up and sniffs at him. But there is no sign of a party or dinner table or guests. In a corridor he runs into old Baroness von Merkens. She is carrying a tray laden with food.

MOTHER   Carry the tray for me, will you. Thank you. This is my supper, you see. Lindhorst, who knows the world, says that old harlots have a morbid desire to satisfy their mouths and stomachs. Are you sure you wouldn't like something?

JOHAN   Isn't there to be a party tonight? I was invited.

MOTHER   Not that I know of. No, no, don't go. Please help me off with my stockings. You don't like touching me, I feel that plainly. I can't make you out. Veronica Vogler has come. Look at my feet, my dear artist. Have you ever seen younger and firmer arches? Take a good look. Look at my heel! So nice and smooth. Such strong toes and such pretty nails. Kiss my foot! You can very well do that. That's the way! Now you're being pleasant. I'll tell you where she is. Look in the west gallery. She was there five minutes ago at any rate. This is a good wine. (*Laughs.*) If you see Mr. Heerbrand, please ask him to come to me.

The west gallery. A very long, low room with windows opening onto the park. The twilight flows over the walls and family portraits. The faint sound of a harpischord can be heard. Baron von Merkens comes slowly toward Johan. He is dressed entirely in black and his face wears a gentle expression. Johan apologizes for having mistaken the day. The baron listens with lowered eyelids. After a moment's silence he begins to speak in a scarcely audible voice.

VON MERKENS   You are always welcome, my dear friend. You come, you stay, you go—you're at perfect liberty. Let's be quite frank. You've come in search of Veronica Vogler. I should perhaps mention, before you meet her, that she has been my mistress for some years. People have been kind enough to tell me in detail of your time together in the past. I can assure you that I suffer. This evening I shall stand by your bed. Every word, every kiss, every movement of your bodies—nothing will be spared me.

Johan leaves him and hurries on in the direction of the harpsichord music. Von Merkens shouts something. Johan turns around. The baron has walked up the wall to the ceiling and is standing like a fly, head downward, apparently without the slightest inconvenience. He takes a few quick steps but stops at the crystal chandelier, fingering its lusters, which tinkle faintly.

  In a small cabinet beyond the gallery the baroness is sitting with an old lady, whom Johan at once recognizes. She is wearing a red silk dress and a large hat with a wide brim, which shadows an extraordinary, ravaged face. At the harpsichord sits a little hunchbacked man, very elegantly dressed. The baroness introduces him as Mr. Kreisler and makes Johan sit beside her on the sofa. Mr. Kreisler begins to play; he is undoubtedly a master.

THE OLD LADY   Oh, this music! I think I shall have to take my hat off to hear better. A master of his instrument! And what an eye for the ladies! Can you imagine? Especially long-legged women like the baroness.

CORINNE   You must go now. Veronica Vogler has waited long enough. I might tell you that she began getting ready for your visit early this morning. She asked my advice about clothes, she washed her hair and she drove Mr. Heerbrand to distraction by occupying their common bathroom for hours and hours. She has grown even more beautiful. Well, you'll see for yourself. (*Sadly.*) And my husband suffers. His jealousy . . . (*Laughs softly.*) And your pathetic little companion! (*In an undertone.*) Three shots, one of them fatal.

Johan stares past the baroness at the old lady, who is starting to take off her hat. Mr. Kreisler stops playing and turns his prominent dark eyes to the ceiling. The baroness takes out a scented handkerchief and presses it to her nose and mouth. When the old lady has taken out her hairpins she lifts the brim; her face comes unstuck and comes away with the hat. She takes out her eyes carefully and lays everything on the table beside her hair. Then she settles herself in the chair. Mr. Kreisler begins to play one of Bach's partitas. Leaning toward Johan the baroness whispers.

CORINNE   What a smell of glue! Though she makes out that everything is synthetic. But it's common or garden glue, that's what it is. She can't fool me.

Mr. Lindhorst comes toward Johan with quick steps, his boyish, rather bloated face lit up by a cheerful smile.

LINDHORST   I knew that you would come at last. We know a trick or two, don't we? Let's see now if we're presentable. Veronica Vogler is an exacting woman, as you know. How pale you are, my dear fellow! You look a sight. Your lips are as blue as if you'd been eating blueberries. We must touch them up. A nice cupid's bow and a sensually swelling underlip are very titillating. Your eyes are bloodshot and swollen. Dab them with this. Now we'll draw a couple of lines in the corner of the eye. A shadow on the eyelid? No? Well, we mustn't overdo it. But a little fresher color in the face won't do any harm. There! You look quite passable. You can borrow my dressing gown. It suits you. Or wait! Silk pajamas are the thing for trysts of this kind. Now for some scent. No? You prefer to smell of yourself. Of course. Each one has his own odor. But a little whiff of perfume all the same. I knew it! Now slippers. There you are. Take a look in the mirror. You are yourself and yet not yourself. The ideal conditions for a lovers' meeting. Here is her door.

Lindhorst claps him on the shoulder. As he raises his arm, huge wings sprout from his shoulders, and below his trouser legs powerful black claws and a pair of bird legs can be seen. Flapping his wings noisily, he rises from the floor, flies around the room, and sails out through the open balcony door. Time and again he squawks like a pheasant.
    Johan pounds on the door, but no one answers. He enters a fairly

large room, entirely furniture. In the middle of the floor stand a couple of trestles. Over these lie some planks. On this primitive bier rests a body covered by a sheet.

He stands for a few moments at the door, bewildered. Then, driven by an irresistible desire, he goes over to the bier, lifts the sheet and exposes Veronica's face. Her very pale lips are slightly parted and an even row of white teeth glitter inside the soft opening of the mouth. The thick hair is combed in a simple coiffure, and in her small, well-shaped ears are a couple of thin gold rings. He draws the sheet from her body. Raising his hand, he touchs her forehead, her cheeks, her neck, chin, and shoulders. Her breasts, the curve of the hip, the tuft of hair covering the genitals, the long, thick thighs.

Suddenly she sits up, opening her legs. Laughing, she throws her arms around his neck and kisses him. She leans over him and he kisses her breasts. She takes his head between her hands and kisses his lips. Then he hears stifled giggles. He sees that the others have come into the room. In the dim light they look like big insects with black, bulging eyes and dark, gleaming limbs. They seem grave and expectant. The laughter, which can be heard all the time, comes from some invisible creatures somewhere high up under the arched roof.

JOHAN The limit has at last been reached. The glass is shattered, but what do the splinters reflect? The void has finally burst the thin shell and meets—the void? In that case what a triumph for the void.

Alma and Johan's house. It is afternoon, as at the beginning of the story. Alma is sitting at the table, looking at the visitor.

ALMA Yes, he fired three shots. One of them grazed my arm. I still have a small scar. I fell over in sheer fright and thought it better to lie still. He came right up to me and whispered: "Alma, Alma." I suppose he thought he had shot me dead. I heard him pacing up and down around the house. Then he ran off toward the path. I got up and went inside, washed the blood off and put on a bandage, then I hid the gun and sat down to wait. He was gone some minutes. Then he came running back. I hid, to be on the safe side. He looked demented. He strode around the room, talking to himself. Then he took out the diary and began to write. He wrote for several hours. In the forenoon he packed his satchel and went off into the woods. I thought I'd better follow him in case he did himself an injury.

Then Alma tells the following story, which I'll try to reproduce as correctly as possible.

The light is as gray as ashes and the flies from the swamp sting my sweating arms and face. Someone says my name in a low, sad voice. I look about, swatting at the insects, and say, "Yes, here I am," several times. A bird swoops above my head, croaking.

Then I catch sight of Johan. He is huddling behind the stump of a tree, trying to hide, but quite visible. His eyes are misty with pain and fear, and his lips are trembling. Sobbing, he stretches out his hands. Several fingers are broken and his arms have sores on them. I crouch down beside him. We remain sitting together like this, incapable of getting any farther.

Dusk comes quickly. The shadows between the trees blacken into thick darkness. Patches of red and blazing yellow appear in the gray sky. The pounding of the sea can be heard like the strokes of a muffled bell. A nightingale begins to sing, sharply and persistently. Now and then there is flutter of invisible wings. I doze off. When I wake he is no longer there. I go in among the trees, wandering about at random.

In a glade faintly illumined by the twilight a horde of shadows move silently, darting this way and that, suddenly swallowed up by the darkness, the next moment discernible again. They run, crawl, dance, and crouch, lifting their arms above their heads, talking together inaudibly, gesticulating, vanishing again. Now the glade is almost deserted, now swarming with life. Colorless, quivering, floating. A smell of foul water rises from the swamp. The nightingale's song, sharp and churring, never stops.

Then I catch sight of him again. He is standing in the middle of the glade. His white shirt and light-colored pants are stained and torn. He stands with his head bent and arms hanging.

A large human-looking bird like a pheasant goes up and pecks at his neck. A black stream of blood wells up; he lifts his broken hands to staunch the flow but lets them fall. A faint, tinkling laughter ripples through the floating, streaming flock. Voices—low, murmuring but distinct—begin to be heard.

VOICES   As long as you stand you may live.
When you fall it's all over for you.
As long as you've the strength to keep upright.
Keep standing!
Don't be afraid.

A lean woman with thick, black, piled-up hair and brown skin as dry as parchment clings to his back and begins tearing at his shirt. The big pheasant closes in on him in narrowing circles, its sharp beak open and its eyeballs turned stiffly to the sides. Now and then it gives a faint hiss. The voices are heard again.

VOICES   Lie down and it will be quicker.
Lie down and you won't have to suffer.
Keep standing and we might get tired.
Keep standing, keep standing, keep standing.
Attack us and tear us to pieces.
Have you no sense of humor?
Can't you take a joke?
Haven't you a tongue in your head?
(There is tinkling, whispering laughter.)
He can't talk because I've made mincemeat of his tongue.
He can't hear because I've torn his ears apart and plugged up the hole with a nail.
He can't see because I've picked out his eyes.
He can't piss because I've nicked him and I think he's a bit swollen.
He can't sit down because he has a pebble in his ass.
But he stands there thinking!
Are you thinking or just being lazy?

The pheasant gurgles with laughter. Then it shuts its beak with a snap and pecks. The voices are heard again.

VOICES   He's falling, he's falling.

The old lady raises her voice. Her red dress gleams faintly in all the grayness; her face under the big, wide-brimmed hat is a white, bobbing patch on the thin neck.

The shadows stop moving. Some disintegrate as if unable to bear the stillness, some fumble for branches and big flowers, others collapse in gray heaps. Lindhorst spreads out his wings and floats up into a low tree with thick branches and thin foliage. The man in the glade now appears to be alone—in the dusk, in the wood, by the sea. The nightingale's churring keeps on and on.

Johan sways to and fro, breathing in shuddering gasps, turning his disfigured face this way and that. I try to run to him, but cannot move. I try to scream, but no sound comes out.

He begins to sink to the ground; slowly his knees bend, his back crooks, his head is thrust forward in an effort to balance his body. He gropes for support. Then he drops to his knees, his chin plows through the moss, his arms flap helplessly, his legs kick.

At the same instant the tumult breaks loose. The shadows grow dense, flitting out of the darkness, out of the air, the night sky, the trees, the rocks, the wind. The white body whirls in the air, is tossed on high, and drops back to the bubbling moss. Shreds of clothing fly in all directions, pale limbs gleam and vanish.

In a few moments the little glade is silent and empty, washed clean in the dawn light. Not a trace. Not even a bloodstain. Only a gentle wind and the silent, steady autumn rain. I return to the house. On the way, I find his satchel with the diary.

The house is bathed in evening light. Alma is sitting heavily, leaning forward with her arms on the table.

ALMA There's one thing I've been puzzling over. Are you in a hurry? I'd like to ask something. It's this: Isn't it so that a woman who lives for a long time together with a man at last comes to be like that man? I mean, she loves him and tries to think as he does and see as he does. They say that it can change people. Was that why I began seeing those others? Or were they there after all? I mean, if I had loved him less and not bothered so much about everything around him, would I have been able to protect him better? Or was it because I didn't love him *enough* that I grew jealous? Was that why those cannibals, as he called them . . . was that why we came to such terrible grief? If I hadn't . . . if I had been able . . . oh, I can't express what I mean. I thought I was so close to him. Sometimes he said that he, too, felt close to me—once he said it quite definitely. If only I could have been with him the whole time . . . I've been wondering so much about it all . . . There are such a lot of questions. Sometimes I don't know which way to turn, and I get quite . . .

THE PASSION OF ANNA

PART ONE

My name is Andreas Winkelman. I am forty-eight. I remember it
was a sultry October day. I was sitting on the roof of my ramshackle
house, repairing it as well as I could, for after the last rain it had
started leaking in earnest. When I glanced up from my work, three
suns hung over the sea. There was not a breath of air—everything
was utterly still and silent. I lit my pipe and sat for a long time
watching the phenomenon. Then a dark cloud appeared from the
west and covered the suns; at last the wind stirred. The afternoon
drew in. A dog barked. The sheep moved solemnly across the moor.
Down on the road Daniel was carting a load of straw, his old horse
jogging along. I climbed down from my lofty perch and went into
the kitchen to make some coffee. The news on the radio told of various kinds of misfortune, but the announcer said nothing about my
three suns.

An hour or so later I saw the group—a man and two women—for
the first time. They were following the road by the sea. They
walked slowly; one of the women moved with difficulty, limping and
supporting herself with a stick. The man looked vaguely Jewish. He
seemed about my age. The two women, apparently very elderly,

were conspicuously elegant. I couldn't hear any conversation; they walked along in silence, deep in thought. As I had passed them, I got off my bicycle and observed them carefully. The lame woman stopped, as though to rest. The others checked their steps, the man asked her something, and she shook her head. The sun had just set, leaving a flaming band above the forest.

My idea was to put the house in order for the winter, so once I repaired the roof, I began work on the steps. I've no knack whatsoever for such activities, but the work itself gives me a feeling of satisfaction. I was hammering and sawing so mightily that I didn't notice at first that someone stood watching me.

She introduced herself: Anna Fromm. She asked whether she might use the phone for an urgent call. Their telephone had been out of order for several days. I showed her where it was, then went out and sat on the steps. I could hear her voice. It sounded calm at first, then more and more upset; then there was silence. Afer a minute or so her stick tapped on the floor, and she opened the door. "I found out what the call cost," she said, holding out a note. I gave her the change.

Her face was set, but she had been crying. She thanked me and went toward the forest. Her right leg was stiff and she moved with difficulty. I sat for a long time looking at my hands, until I found I was shivering with cold in the bleak autumn day. I couldn't help laughing at myself.

Then Verner turned up in his old truck. He had promised to deliver some timber and a few other things. While we unloaded them, our talk turned to the three strangers: an architect named Vergérus and his wife had bought a house down at Ottar, which they had renovated. Anna Fromm was staying with them. She had been in a tragic car crash over a year ago. We remembered: it was a horrible accident. Her husband and son had been killed. She herself had been badly injured.

Later in the afternoon I discovered that Anna Fromm had left her handbag on the table by the telephone. In the bag lay a folded letter which obviously had been read many times. It was dated eighteen months earlier. I read it:

Dearest Anna.

I cannot live with you any longer. I have been pushing this truth aside for some time, because I love you. But I cannot, and will not, live with you any more. I don't believe in any new attempts, as neither you nor I seriously want to change. I suppose it's our mental defects that bring out the worst in each other. It is best that we don't meet. I will only give in, as despite everything I am in love with you. But I *don't want* to give in, because I know that we shall only involve ourselves in new complications which in their turn will bring on terrible mental disturbances, as well as physical and mental acts of violence. I think it would be a good idea if our lawyers could talk over the practical problems. You will think I'm a coward for writing to you and not talking to you. The reason is simply that when I'm together with you I grow weak and do what you want me to do. I ask you therefore not to get in touch with me. Andreas.

I made my way to their house—a large, white-plastered farmhouse carefully restored. Mrs. Eva Vergérus opened the door. She thanked me very much on behalf of her friend and said she was sorry that Anna, who felt a slight cold coming on, had gone to bed. Mr. Vergérus appeared in the doorway and kindly asked me to come in and have a brandy. I declined, saying that the lamp on my bicycle was broken. Vergérus then offered to drive me home, but I still declined. His wife smiled and said she hoped we would meet on a more suitable occasion. I wished them good night. On the way home my bicycle struck a stone, I fell off and grazed the palm of my right hand.

A few days later, I was on the way to Deeprock to fish. The Vergérus's car was standing at the crossroads: it was apparently empty. As I came closer, I saw Mrs. Vergérus lying on the front seat with her eyes shut. I was about to withdraw when I felt a sudden anxiety —perhaps she was ill, unconscious, dead. I opened the car door cautiously and looked at her: she was asleep, with her mouth half open and a worried expression on her face—like a child left all on its own. I touched her shoulder and she woke at once, but lay still.

"Excuse me for waking you. I was anxious. I thought you were ill or unconscious or something."

"It doesn't matter. I sleep very badly at night, you see. So I just drop off sometimes during the day."

I said goodbye quickly and she started the car.

The next day I was out in the forest gathering pine cones with which to smoke the flounder I had caught. It was drizzling. I heard a strange sound, but at first I paid it no attention, as I thought it came from a bird or from the sheep grazing at the bottom of the slope. But the sound grew more and more peculiar, and at last I began to trace it. After a while I found the cause—someone had hung a puppy in a tree. It was still alive, and as I came up, it tried to bite my hands. I managed to cut it down and to free its neck from the noose. The animal, already half dead, twitched and jerked. I thought I heard someone running off, but I may have been mistaken. I took the puppy home, and by degrees it recovered.

One morning I was wallpapering my bedroom, which had been in a deplorable state for a long time. The dog, which I had named Oscar, was curled up on my bed, which I had pulled out to the middle of the floor. The rain was pouring down. Suddenly Oscar started barking. From the window, I saw Elis Vergérus running across the yard. He knocked at the door, and I went and opened it. He apologized; he had been caught in the rain, having thoughtlessly gone out without a raincoat—the early morning sky had been clear. I asked him into the kitchen, where it was warm. He took off his jacket and hung it over a chair by the stove. I made some coffee and we talked. He mentioned casually that his hobby was photography. I asked if there was any special kind of photography that interested him. He replied that he was very keen on registering all aspects of human life, but that he was, of course, a mediocre amateur and his collections were limited. I asked whether he had photographed the three suns. He shook his head; all at once he was impatient and his thoughts seemed elsewhere. I offered to lend him my raincoat. He nodded acceptance, got up quickly, extended a soft, dry hand, and thanked me for my hospitality. Then, putting on my raincoat, he strode away between the pools of water.

They had been away from their house in November and December, but came back just before Christmas. I ran across them here and there—in the shops, when I cycled out onto the moor, or stood down by the stream fishing. We began to greet each other like old acquaintances. One day Mrs. Vergérus got stuck with her car in a snowdrift. My helping her out resulted in an invitation to dinner. Not quite knowing why, I accepted. I went home and shaved, although it was only Friday. I put on a dark suit, white shirt, and my best tie, and thought myself quite presentable.

They had a lovely home, furnished in soft colors and very good taste, an exquisite blend of austereness and refinement, of old and new. They themselves were warm, friendly, and openhearted. The food and drink exhilarated me. Anna's and Eva's beauty, and Elis's kindness and attention banished my reserve. I felt a sudden affection for these people. Late at night I was invited to the guest room, where I sank into a big, soft bed.

I woke in the gray light of dawn with a vague sense of anguish. It was completely silent, after the noise and storm of the evening. I lay there thirsty and in a cold perspiration. Suddenly I heard sighs and weeping. It was a woman's voice. Perhaps it was Anna. But as the voice sounded unfamiliar, it could also have been someone else. Then I heard a man's voice speaking quietly and comfortingly, but also commandingly, decisively. A cry of pain: "Andreas! Andreas!" I realized now that it was Anna calling out. Then silence once more. Quick footsteps. A door was opened and shut.

The same morning Vergérus invited me to his studio. It was in one of the outbuildings and consisted of one huge room with a skylight and bare, coarse-timbered walls. There was another big window facing north. Photography equipment and lamps rested on shelves. A few odd chairs, a linen screen, a simple bed, and some indefinable objects occupied the room. On one of the end walls, a small figurehead was mounted, chafed and faded. Along one side wall, there were other shelves with big, numbered cardboard boxes. Elis went over to the boxes and drew out one or two. In them were photographs, as well as quantities of pictures cut out of newspapers and magazines, packed and catalogued.

"At first I collected all kinds of pictures. Those I had taken myself and those I found in newspapers, magazines, old albums, and secondhand bookshops. Collecting these pictures became a passion, in fact. They were always about people, people in all situations. In this box, for instance, you have people eating, all categories. Nearly a thousand pictures. Here you have people in the grip of violent emotions—that is this section of boxes with different subsections. At one time I collected only pictures of violence and acts of violence. Here you have people asleep with the subsection dead people. As you see, I have catalogued according to behavior. It's a completely irrational classification, which seems to me just as pointless as the collecting itself. If you like, some time we can look at my pornographic pictures. There are between twenty and thirty thousand. I haven't counted them and most of them are rubbish. Only about ten or twelve are any good."

As he talked he pulled boxes out, pushed boxes in, and thumbed through photographs, all with the same slightly irritated indifference. It became a thick, strange movement of human life. He laughed and shrugged.

"That row over there is only faces, closeups. Come and have a look. I've taken those pictures myself and some of them are interesting. I was going to ask if I might take a series of you, too. Would you mind?"

I said something to the effect that it would be an honor and that I had all the time in the world. He nodded, and looked as if he had immediately forgotten the whole matter. He skimmed through a bundle of pictures and handed me some with a smile.

"Here's something that might interest you: Anna Fromm, at the age of twenty-three. Happily married. Seven years before the catastrophe."

I saw an open, childish face; large, smooth, unmarked features; a sensitive, smiling mouth. Anna Fromm, twenty-three years old. (Who was it now that dragged herself along through existence under the same name?) Elis smiled and I felt his eyes on me. I protected myself at once by asking whether he had any pictures of her husband. He nodded and pulled out another box. "Here's your namesake." The pictures were taken two days before his death: a big, dark man with a broad face, smiling eyes, generous mouth, and a big, turned-up nose. I asked Elis what this Andreas was like.

"To tell the truth, I don't really know. He was generally regarded as a scientific genius. He was a mixture of warmhearted good nature and ice-cold ruthlessness. When it suited him he was utterly sincere, and when it didn't suit him he made up any conceivable lie. He was entirely enclosed within himself but never seemed egocentric or aloof. From what I can make out, he was an out-and-out sensualist, he loved food and drink and women with the same genuine enthusiasm. Oh yes, we had been friends since our school days, but I can't say that I knew him. For Anna he was a catastrophe, for obvious reasons. She loved him to the point of madness. I have never seen anything like it, though I may have read about it in literature. I gather he also loved her in his extraordinary way. I don't really know. You can't stop anyone from a single suffering and that's what makes you so tired."

He tossed the photographs into the drawer and closed it with an impatient gesture.

"Anyway, I'm not qualified to judge. For a year my wife was his mistress. I'm not complaining. It was quite aboveboard. She kept nothing from me and I accepted it. One day she left him. I still don't know why. I haven't dared to ask. What was I going to say now? Oh yes. I can tell you that Eva . . . I'd like to say that Eva . . . Eva has an extraordinary mental strength, although you wouldn't think so to see her. Eva and Anna have been inseparable friends for many years. After the accident, when Anna was left alone—she has only an old, insufferable mother—Eva took her under her wing. Well, that's how it is. Now you know."

One day I was plodding through the newly fallen snow. There had been a violent storm and now a thaw had set in—a silent, dripping grayness. I made my way slowly across the moor. It was heavy going, as in a dream, and the sweat sprang out under my shirt. The mist lay thick over the sea. In the distance I heard the hoarse voices of the foghorns. Everything was motionless, damp: the trees shiny and black, with their branches trailing over the snow or cutting the colorless sky. My heart was pounding. I stopped, stood still, listened. Nothing. No one. I shouted, loud and inarticulately. Then I began to call my own name: "Andreas! Andreas!" Then I started coughing and clearing my throat. At last I reeled off all the curses, all the four-letter words I could think of, until I was hoarse. The tension relaxed then and I laughed to myself. Nobody had heard me, not even the echo.

(Andreas)

The world rolls over me. I've no shelter any more. I've no one to turn to in protest, no one to accuse, not even myself. I am helplessly exposed. I cannot exorcise or transform what I see and hear. It goes on incessantly hour after hour, it bleeds, gurgles, screams, creeps, and stinks. I look on dispirited, frightened, paralyzed.

PART TWO

The snow had all gone, and although the sun shone every day it was bitterly cold. I had been living more or less in isolation for about five weeks. One day Eva Vergérus came to see me. She looked embarrassed but purposeful and gave a little forced laugh.

"I've been alone for three days and am bored to tears. So this morning when I got up I thought: I'll go and see Andreas Winkelman. He can only turn me out. Would you like to show me your house?"

We looked through it.

"I admire your being able to live alone. I simply must have company. Just these few days have been terribly boring. Anna promised to come, but phoned at the last minute and said she couldn't. She is to have another operation on her leg. The fourth. Poor Anna. It was a car crash. Both her husband and their little boy were killed. Anna was in the hospital for several months."

We were standing in my wife's ceramics workshop. I hadn't touched anything since she left.

"Are you divorced? Forgive me, that was tactless. Do you think she will come back? Don't you ever long for her? Forgive me for putting my foot in it like that."

Throwing her arms around me, she kissed me on the cheek. Then she laughed and shook her head. But her eyes were sad.

We ate a good meal and drank rather a lot of wine. She inspected my phonograph records and played some old-fashioned dance music.

"Elis hates it when I dance. He says it embarrasses him."

She danced by herself, gravely introspective like a child. The sun was now low in the sky; it shone through the small windows and dyed everything burning yellow. Suddenly she sat down, looking sad.

"Elis is awfully tired of me. I don't know how to put it. I'm a small part of his big general weariness. The difference is just that . . . The world is indifferent to Elis's sarcasm. But I'm not. No. I wish I could pay him back. But I can't think of anything. I don't know what to do, you see. Elis is a fantastic person and I . . . The worst of it all is that I love him. I mean *love*. There's no other word for it. I can't even show him my love. *What is to become of us, Andreas?* Why do we grow like this? What is it that destroys us bit by bit? What is this deadly poison that corrodes the best in us, leaving only the shell?"

She yawned and blinked, sighed. Then she dropped onto my old sofa.

"Lord, how sleepy the wine has made me! May I lie here and have a nap? It would be so nice. Or am I disturbing you? I haven't slept all night, only wandered about."

I fetched a blanket and pillow from the bedroom, spread the blanket over her, and arranged the pillow under her head.

The puppy, which from the outset had been seized with affection for this stranger, jumped up beside her and crept down under the blanket. Eva talked babyish nonsense to it for a few minutes. Suddenly they were asleep. I turned off the phonograph and went in the kitchen to wash up. The sun was shining, the yellow was changing to red. I felt a light, warm gaiety.

Now and then I went in and looked at my guest. She was in a deep sleep, unmoving, with her open hands turned upward near her head. The light was fading. I lit the lamp and sat down at the table with a book. After an hour or so she woke up.

"I promised to phone Elis. He's going abroad tomorrow. May I use the phone? Where's my handbag? I wrote down the number. He's having dinner with a friend."

With a worried expression she groped about in her very large, chaotic bag, at last found what she was looking for, and phoned.

"I'm sorry to call so late, my dear. Had you already sat down to dinner? Shall I ring a little later? No? I dozed off, you see, and slept for several hours. Yes, everything's all right. I met Andreas when I was out for a walk. No, I'm alone. Not at all, dearest. Everything's fine. Only don't be cross with me. Have a good time now. Yes. Yes. Yes, I promise. No, you needn't. Yes, I promise. Write to me. Just a line. No, I'm alone, I said. Take care of yourself. Are you coming on Thursday for sure? I'll meet you. Yes, I will. Goodbye, darling. Don't forget your little girl."

She said the last in a distressed voice. She put the phone down and sat hunched up for a while, with the puppy in her lap. Then she looked at me in confusion.

"You must have thought it was silly of me to say I was alone. But he'd be furious if he knew I was here. Not that he's jealous. Or maybe he is jealous after all. He has been given a fantastic commission: to design a civic center in Milan. It's a great feather in his cap. *He* is successful!"

She said the last with an indescribable tone of pride and desperation. She came up to me and kissed me on the mouth. Her face was utterly bare. She caressed my face over and over again. We stood in the twilight of the silent room, letting time go by.

"Andreas! Andreas! It's so hard to realize one day that you're meaningless. That you live for nothing. That you're not even living for your own sake. That no one needs you, though there you are, wanting to give of yourself. I suppose it's my own fault, but it's paralyzing. I want to accomplish so much and I make plans. Then I talk to Elis and he says, 'No, you should do this and this, don't do that.' Then it all ends in smoke . . . no, I mustn't blame Elis, it's not fair. Everything I touch goes wrong. But Elis is so . . . no, I shouldn't blame Elis. I shouldn't . . ."

When night came she was sleepless. She wandered about the kitchen, lighted the kerosene heater, and wrapped her fur coat around her. Her face was now strained and severe, her eyes were dark with pent-up suffering. Turning toward me, she made a warding-off gesture.

"No, you go in and sleep. I'll come later. This is nothing to worry about. I'll just walk about. I do every night."

An hour later she was back in the bedroom. She took off her coat and got into bed, cuddling close against me.

"I've taken two strong shots, so I'll be asleep in a few minutes. Sometimes I've such an awful desire to take the lot. Once I was pregnant. Then I couldn't sleep at all. They put me in the hospital so that I could get some sleep. They said they'd put me to sleep for several days. By mistake I was given too strong an injection. I didn't sleep, but the child died. Elis was with me that time. We cried together. It has never happened before or since. I never had any children after that. It's just as well. It's better that way."

The phone was ringing. I don't know how long I had been asleep. Eva lay unmoving beside me. Ring after ring. At last I answered. It was Elis. His voice sounded gray.

"I'm sorry to be ringing so late. It's Elis Vergérus. I've tried and tried to phone home, but there's no answer. Eva is usually awake all night, so I'm rather worried that she doesn't answer. I'm sorry to trouble you, but would you mind awfully going down to see if everything is all right? Tell Eva I was worried. She needn't call me. Then perhaps you'd phone me as soon as possible."

She was standing by the window and the sun shone hard on her face. The eyes were veiled with tiredness. She seemed to want to reveal herself, expose herself to the light and to me. The big clock ticked and struck a single tone. The immobility of the winter day.

"Now you can see how ugly I am. Look at me, Andreas. Have you ever been to bed with a more dreary love partner? Say I'm wrong."

"You're wrong."

"You've been so kind to me. I'm going to miss you terribly. I want to be here with you."

She hid her face in her hand, bent her head in a humble movement that I cannot describe. I was seized with a painful tenderness.

I said that we'd meet soon, that she wasn't to worry, that she mustn't be afraid. She listened with a faint smile, deprecating, mistrustful. Suddenly she kissed me lightly and said goodbye.

"Will you call me?" I asked, feeling unexpectedly forsaken.

"I'll call you."

"Or perhaps you'll write to me. If you'd rather."

"No, I'll call."

"When do you think you'll be back?"

"Next time I'll probably come with Elis and Anna. For a few weeks at Easter."

"Can't you come here by yourself before that? Just for a few days."

In this way, talking and asking anxious questions, I went outside with her to the front of the house.

"We'll see, I don't know, we'll see," she said. She looked at me in surprise, smiling faintly. "Now I must hurry, or I'll miss the ferry."

She glanced at her watch. Then she put her arms around me and we kissed. As she drove off in her little red car, which gleamed between the trees on the forest path, I had a feeling of loss which hurt physically. My hard-won and well-defended solitude suddenly seemed paltry. The puppy sat behind me on the steps, crying openly. We went inside, as it was bitterly cold. The house was empty.

It became clear that a madman was running amuck on the island. One morning Verner found eight of his sheep killed and horribly mutilated. They lay around the feeding place, their eyes gouged out, bellies slit open, legs half chopped off. The police came, made an examination, and asked questions. It turned out that other cases of savage cruelty to animals had occurred during the last few months. Some cows had had their tails broken, three or four hens had been found torn to pieces. For my part, I thought I had better tell the police how I had found my puppy. They noted it all down and went off. I helped Verner and his wife to bury the bodies of the sheep. She wept. Verner said nothing. The sea was gray and motionless.

One day a few weeks before Easter I agreed to let Elis Vergérus photograph me. I went to his studio in the morning and we set to work. He seemed utterly disinterested. He wandered around the room smoking, now and then taking a picture. The camera stood unchanged on a tripod right in front of me. I sat on a chair feeling ridiculous (and, in a way I can't explain even to myself, humiliated). We chatted, that is to say, Elis talked.

"I met one of the police yesterday on the ferry. He says they have no trace but that the local people suspect Johan Andersson out at Skir. He has been in a mental hospital and that alone is suspicious. Also, he lives alone, totally isolated, never speaks, has no friends, no animals. I photographed him a few years ago. He was quite sociable then, but he got mixed up in some lawsuit, which he lost. It was such a blow to him that he isolated himself."

Elis rummaged in one of his drawers and took out a bunch of photographs which he handed to me: Andersson has a hypersensitive, mournful face with deep-set, pale, childlike eyes and a remarkable drawn-down mouth as if in a rigid fit of weeping. A large aquiline nose. Sunken cheeks covered with stubble. I noticed that Elis took a series of pictures while I was looking at the old man's face.

"I've been thinking over your finances, Andreas, and I think I can help you. To begin with, you need a proper loan to set you on your feet, so that you can pay off your debts and have them all in one quarter. I'll put my name to the necessary papers. My lawyer can then draw up a plan for paying the money back in installments."

I expressed my gratitude and Elis took a few pictures in passing. He was friendly, almost warm, at any rate sincerely cordial.

"Don't be afraid, everything will work out for the best. There's only one problem: you must without fail earn a little money, for living expenses and paying off the debt. Have you any suggestions?"

I replied that I had no suggestions, that I had a horror of letting myself in for any form of organized existence. Elis listened attentively, took a couple of pictures, reloaded his camera, and changed the lighting.

"Well, for the time being there's no danger. You can type, can't you? While you're thinking it over perhaps you'd like to type out my notes. I've made a gigantic survey of this civic center in Milan."

I replied that I thought it was a good idea. At the same time I felt frightened and ill. Elis took a whole series of pictures. Only then did I notice that he had been drinking the whole time.

"For God's sake, don't think I imagine that I reach into the human soul with this photography. I can only register an interplay and counterplay of thousands of forces, large and small. Then you look at the picture and give rein to your imagination. That woman lies just for the pleasure of it, that person is a future corpse, that boy will meet with disaster. Everything is nonsense, games, fancies. You cannot read another person with the slightest claim to certainty. Not even brutal physical pain always gives a reaction."

He showed me a picture of Eva. She was actually smiling, with wide eyes and a relaxed face.

"She didn't know I took that picture. I was standing inside a dark room and photographed her through the window out toward the terrace. She had just got one of her migraine attacks."

I looked at the familiar face and for some reason felt furious. I heard myself say that it was damned interesting.

There was a tap at the door. Eva hurried in, bringing the mail and papers, which she put on a small table. She still had her coat and hat on. We greeted each other in a friendly but impersonal way. Turning to her husband, she said that Falkman was outside, wanting to know which thermostats were out of order. Elis left us.

"Andreas, my dear, I only want you to know that I'm not angry with you or jealous or anything like that. Anna has told me about you two. I think she's very much in love. I think so, though it's very hard to say anything about Anna's feelings. I'm so fond of you both. I'm so fond of you, Andreas. I think of you often. I think of you all the time."

She got up and came quickly over to me, putting her rain-wet hand to my eyes, my mouth, and my brow.

"Your face is almost obliterated. How much longer must you run away? You can't in any case escape."

She smelled of tears and insomnia. We smiled at each other, like two conspirators in a perilous situation.

"You must be careful with Anna. I can't say what I mean. But you must be careful. Don't misunderstand me."

Then she made a quick gesture to push me away. Elis was in the doorway.

His face was wet with the rain. His pallor looked as if it were covered with tiny drops of cold perspiration. His eyes looked bigger. He was struggling with a rage that he could hardly control. Suddenly he laughed.

"It's always trifles that make me lose my temper. Shall we go on with the séance, or are you tired, Andreas? When will lunch be ready?"

"In about an hour," Eva replied, going quietly out of the studio and closing the door behind her. Elis lighted a cigar and went over to the window. He stood there for several minutes without speaking.

"You've been in prison, haven't you?"

I replied that I had been in prison for tax evasion.

"How could you be so stupid?"

"I panicked, and I had bad advisers. If you *must* know, I was convicted at the same time of forging checks. And I drove a car under the influence of liquor. And struck a policeman."

"Have you a guilty conscience?"

"Should I have?"

Elis came up with the bottle of whiskey and poured some out. He was very close to me. I looked him straight in the eyes.

"And now you slink away like a whipped cur," Elis said.

"I *am* a whipped cur."

"Do you bite?"

"I don't think so."

Anna was in the doorway. She was wearing a bright green dress and her hair was done up in a high knob. She was smiling and gay. Elis got up and greeted her with a compliment. He suddenly seemed quite sober. Anna asked if the photography had gone well. I assured her with a laugh that it was awful. Elis said jokingly that I ought to be an actor and that I have a very interesting face. Anna asked why I didn't say anything about her dress. I replied that I was stunned, but that it was very beautiful and suited her wonderfully. Elis had resumed his photography. Anna moved about the room, still smiling. I asked her whether she'd mind sitting over by the camera, so that I would have something beautiful to look at while Elis photographed me. She did so with pleasure, sitting on a high stool, like a bar stool, and lighting a cigarette. She sat very gracefully, with one hand on her hip and her legs crossed, observing me with a smile.

"Don't look so serious! Look at me and smile. That's it. Now enjoy it. Think that I am pretty and Elis is amusing. I know we're getting an awfully good lunch, I have been spying in the kitchen. Eva has seen to everything herself. Can't you take some pictures of Andreas and me together? Oh, go on, Elis, please do!"

She jumped down from the stool and sat beside me, taking my hand, turning my face to hers.

"Now try and look a little bit in love, Andreas, my sweet. That's it. Take a picture now. Hurry, Elis!"

Friday, the fifth of April. Martin Luther King had been murdered. An endless twilight hung over the sea. The heavy white moon of Easter. There would be stars in the ice-clear air. Anna and I went for a walk across the moor. From the water's edge could be heard a constant chatter of migrating birds. The eye of the lighthouse winked. Out in the protective semidarkness of the moor the sheep were lying with their newborn lambs, primeval animals, unmoving, with yellow eyes. Anna walked beside me, holding her hand against my arm.

"I long for God, long to be able to kneel down. Sometimes I pray merely because it feels unbearable not to pray. I find it so hard to live without God. I'm not a believer. I *can't* believe. But I know that when I say there's no God, I'm only saying half the truth and denying something important that I don't understand or don't want to understand. For me, it's insoluble. No Christ can console me. Do you understand me, Andreas?"

Just before we went to bed I switched on the ancient TV set. The riots raged in humming, snowing pictures. We stood in front of the set, staring at the fiery storm and listening to the dry, matter-of-fact comments. Suddenly the screen gave up. It was overwhelmed by darkness, interference, high pressure, and distance. I switched it off and went into the kitchen to get a beer. Anna had a sandwich. Then there was a thud against the pane, as though a soft little ball had been flung against the window.

"It's a bird," Anna said. "Better see if it's all right."

We went out into the cold spring night with a torch. On the paving stones below the window lay a little bird with one wing outspread, still alive but in a bad way.

"We must kill it," Anna said.

I lifted the bird carefully. It hardly moved. I laid it on the step and struck the little head with a stone. Anna dug a hole in the flower bed with her fingers and buried the body. My hand was spattered with tiny flecks of blood and I rinsed it under the tap.

"It couldn't have survived, could it?" Anna asked.

"No, it was too badly injured."

"I wonder why it was out flying like that at night," Anna asked.

"I don't know. Perhaps something scared it."

Anna was worried and brooding; she didn't want to sleep. We sat on the bed with a game of chess between us. After a long silence she began a quiet but pressing interrogation. I defended myself as best I could. The kerosene lamp hissed sleepily.

"Eva is utterly defenseless and can't protect herself. Anyone can do what they like with her."

"She doesn't have to protect herself against me."

"Confess you had an affair when she was staying here alone last autumn."

"Actually we didn't."

"What did you have, then?"

Smiles. She sighed, then struck the quilt with her hand so that the chess pieces leaped up and fell in a muddle.

"What's the time, by the way?"

"Wait, I'll have a look. Half-past one. Aren't you tired?"

"I'm wide awake. Shall I get you a whiskey? Or would you like your pipe?"

She padded around the room, barefoot on the ice-cold floor, with an enormous shawl over her nightgown. She got the bottle out of the cupboard and the pipe from the desk. She filled the pipe, lighted it, and then poured the whiskey. Anna handed me the pipe and glass, gathered up the chess pieces, and started lining them up.

"Love? No. Affinity? No. Truth? Well . . . Affection? Oh, yes. Loyalty? Perhaps. Fidelity? No."

"Tenderness? Yes!"

"I'm going to find out who you are."

"I am no one, Anna. I've made a big effort to wipe out—what shall I call it?—my mental characteristics. That has been my hobby for several years. Oh, yes, I've had another life, if you know what I mean. We lived in this house. My wife worked with her ceramics, I was busy on a scientific survey concerning the geological history of the island. Our little daughter played about and went to school nearby."

"What happened?"

"Nothing, Anna! Absolutely nothing. We got on fairly well. My wife had a show. It was a success. Then she wanted to get away from here. My survey was considered valuable and resulted in a bigger survey, which tied me to this island for another few years. Everything was splendid. But it was the end."

"Where is your family now?"

"I don't really know. My big survey was not as successful as the small one. I gave up research. If you want to know what I do, I can tell you that I exist as a formality. If you try to grab me, I'll drain away between your hands like lukewarm water."

Anna's face was in shadow; her voice sounded faraway.

"I think you're lying. Did you spin the same yarn to poor Eva?"

"She never asked."

"So you did have an affair?"

At that instant the kerosene lamp went out with a sad sigh. We touched each other, groped for each other. I felt her hand on my throat. The grip was merciless. I was seized by a sudden dread of death and freed myself, roughly. She kissed me, laughing silently. We moved downward, inward, toward the darkness.

(Eva)

I couldn't endure it: being conscious, seeing with open eyes, knowing what was going on. So I took the remaining sleeping pills and sank into a deep coma. It was crisscrossed by ghastly dreams. I wanted to wake up but couldn't. On the third day they roused me. By then my existence was changed, I thought that my previous being was a little sister who had died long ago and whom I mourned with sadness but no sense of loss. Now I am learning the language of deaf-mutes. It is a liberation, I'd like to call it a reprieve. I have left the past and exist only in the present.

PART THREE

I have read through what I have written and find it monotonous and sketchy. I keep feeling disgust at the wording, yet I go on. It's as if something were driving me on, perhaps the fancy of a goal. Here all roads run together; here is the root of evil. Thus I can divide guilt and punishment. Is that liberation? I think not. Perhaps I am driven by a more modest hope: a longing for affinity, a secret dream of understanding. Look, here is the splinter, an indecipherable fragment. Pick it up and do what you like with it. But please—go about it carefully. Turn the splinter between your hands and let it grow into a message, an appeal. That is why I go on, all the time doubtful, without a system. Haphazardly.

The road narrowed and twisted. One one side was the moor and the sea, on the other the forest. It was a desolate place with stone walls and a rather deep ditch. Everywhere, there were tiny streams from the melting snows. The sunlight came and went. We stopped the car and walked slowly toward the bend in the road. Anna stopped, looked about her, took a few steps, then stopped again. She climbed over the ditch, and leaned against the stone wall. I could see then that it had been mended. Inside it, one or two trees had been cut down. "Was it here?" I asked stupidly. She nodded.

Later the same afternoon. I own a leaky rowboat and in calm weather one can venture out in it. We went out to put the net down. There was very little wind but the air was cold. Waterfowl could be heard everywhere. The sun was in a bank of mist on the horizon. Anna spoke of her marriage.

"He was fifteen years older than I. We had not known each other very long when we got married. I had lived with one or two men, had even been engaged."

I rowed toward the jetty. The thick red disc of the sun was behind her.

"I fell in love. It was on a trip to Hungary. I was still reading Slavic languages at the university and there was a group of us traveling together. He wasn't supposed to be coming at all, but he was given some commission or a study grant or whatever it was, so he took the opportunity of coming with us. He had just defended his doctor's thesis and been wildly successful. Everyone spoke of him as a genius."

She looked at me with an apologetic smile.

"Six months later we were married. I was already pregnant. Everything was far and above reality, though at the time I didn't understand that. He was so . . ."

We reached the jetty, stepped ashore, and drew the boat up onto the stony beach.

"We lived in complete affinity. We thought the same thoughts and were together in everything. It sounds so absurd and exaggerated when I tell you this. But it's so hard to describe how two people do actually become part of each other. There are only trite words which don't cover the experience at all. Do they?"

We were on the way up to the old house. It looked more dilapidated than ever. Anna walked beside me confidingly. Confidingly? I put my arm around her shoulders. "What was it that happened?" I kept my arm around her shoulders.

"The child was a deep and compound experience—everything to do with the child. Do you know what I mean? I passed my exam and got a position as a teacher. Andreas was given an assistant professorship. Twice a week he went to Uppsala to lecture. We had bought a small house outside town and furnished it by degrees, as we could afford it. Slowly we built up something together. I don't know what to call it. A real security. A security?"

She didn't want to go in. We stood on the steps. I lighted my pipe and looked around me. A great deal needed immediate repair.

I said I was grateful to her for wanting to tell me. I whistled to the dog, and we continued across the snow-free ground. It crunched underfoot. The sun had set, and it was getting cold.

"You'll probably think from this that Andreas and I lived in an ideal marriage with no dissension. But that was not so. It was pretty stormy at times. We were so different, you see. He was warm and gay and always in a good mood and abominably careless."

She put her cold, bare hand in mine.

"No, we had violent quarrels, but we never infected each other with cruelty or suspicion. And we were always completely honest. There wasn't a vestige of pretense in our relationship. Andreas was unfaithful to me once. You didn't think that, did you? Well, he was. But he confessed and told me. I was angry and upset, but I felt that he loved me all the same, so I got over it and we took greater care of each other than ever. The worst thing was once when he left me. But I found out where he was, and he changed his mind and came back. Then we lived closer together than before. We had planned to go abroad for six months—travel about and be together and have a look around. We felt we needed to get away from the humdrum daily routine for a while. During the fall we planned and organized. Then we came out here for the weekend, Andreas and I and our little boy. Eva and Elis had lent us their house. It was on a Sunday. We had just eaten lunch. Andreas wanted to have a nap, but I wanted us to drive up and look at the church ruins. I got my way and we set off. Andreas had had a few drinks, so he let me drive. We were in high spirits. I wasn't driving fast at all. The road was slippery and the car began to skid. Andreas tried to grab the wheel, but the car shot off the road, down into the ditch, through the stone wall, and straight in among the trees. I don't know what happened. When I came to, I wandered about looking at the wreck of a car and at a man who sat there with a great gash in his neck and half his body through the windshield. A little boy lay farther away. He had been hurled out through a door and his head was in a funny position. I remember thinking: What a ghastly accident, fancy there being nobody who can help those poor people. I made my way up onto the road. Slowly I began to feel the pain in one side and in my leg. Then I saw I was covered with blood. The blood was streaming everywhere, I was dragging one foot behind me, and my shinbone was sticking through my stocking. They found us a few hours later. I didn't think life could look like that. I didn't think life could be a daily suffering.

Diligence, cleanliness, and a timid happiness prevailed in my old house. True, the warnings were there *underneath*. They could be glimpsed just below the dark surface of the water like strange, shapeless water creatures that arouse our fear in a primeval and intangible way.

One afternoon we saw old Johan of Skir; he moved like a groping shadow against the white-glistening sea. He was gathering the coarse-smelling seaweed on his wheelbarrow—a heavy load for an old man. Anna asked how he was getting on, if we could help him with anything. The friendly voice made the old man's lackluster eyes water. He shook his head, and merely said that people were being spiteful and nasty to him. They had threatened to kill him for all that cruelty to animals. One day they would, too. He was sure of that. They would kill him, although he was innocent. We helped him pull the barrow home to his cottage. He showed me a scrap of paper. It had come flying through the window with a stone. On the paper was scrawled: "You bloody old animal murderer. We're going to do to you what you did to the animals."

"*Me* cruel to animals!" the old man said with a pitiful smile, an attempt to laugh. He looked for cups, wanting to offer us coffee. I promised him I would phone the police. He looked at me mistrustfully and asked what was the use. The police have already been here.

"Why not get away from here?" I asked helplessly.

"Where could I go?" the old man replied.

The submerged warnings manifested themselves unexpectedly. Anna told me a dream—a long coherent dream she had had at Easter in connection with Martin Luther King's murder. I asked her to write it down or speak it into the tape recorder. She did so. Now, a year later, when I am collecting all this material, I think it is right to insert her dream into the chain. It is a strange experience to hear her slow, hesitant voice.

I was on a stretch of dark water, which was hardly moving. In the boat were some other women and children with pale faces, pinched from lack of sleep. They were well bundled against the cold. The boat scraped against a dilapidated jetty and we got out. A little way up the slope stood a solitary house; a faint light gleamed in a window. The ground in front of the house was stony and surrounded by tumbledown outhouses. An ashen-gray half light hung over the scene and the forest looked black and impenetrable. I recognized the locale and the house—familiar yet strange. A woman stood by the rusty pump, holding two heavy pails. Behind the forest there was a fiery glow, which got brighter and brighter.

I was walking along a sandy road. An icy wind was blowing off the sea. In front of me moved a small, thin figure, hunched against the wind.

"Why are you in such a hurry?"

"I was afraid."

"What are you so afraid of?"

"I must get home before two. No one must be out after two."

"Is it two o'clock already?"

"No, I think it's a quarter past one. But it's nearly dark. It won't get any lighter than this."

"What is that glow over there above the forest?"

"I don't know, I think the forest is on fire."

"How old are you?"

"Eighteen."

"May I come home with you?"

"No, that would never do. We mustn't have guests any more. It's forbidden. We have changed the locks on all the doors."

"Why?"

"I don't know. It just is so."

"Can't you stay for a while?"

"No, I must run."

I was alone on the road. I felt a terrible longing for companionship. For someone's arms around me. For rest. At the same time I had knowledge that this had gone forever, probably squandered through some incredible carelessness. Suddenly I saw a lot of people. They had lighted a fire behind the ruins of the house. Fifteen, twenty women and children had gathered to warm themselves. They stood and sat with their faces turned toward the glow of the fire. Half turned away, and almost by herself, sat a large, lean woman of about sixty. I could not see her face, it was in the shadow. Her shoulders were broad and bony, and she was bareheaded. The thick hair was unkempt and streaked with gray. I could see her hands. They were strong and broad, marked by hard work; a wide wedding ring gleamed faintly in the glow of the fire. She sat leaning forward, her elbows resting on her thighs. The women around her were talking in subdued voices, but none turned to her; she was treated more with a kind of tender respect. I asked in a whisper who the woman was. There was silence, they looked at me with suspicion. I repeated my question: "Who is that woman?"

"We're waiting for a bus that should have come this morning. We've been told that it will be here before midnight, but no one knows for sure when it will come."

"But who is that woman?" I asked for the third time.

"Her son is to be executed. She is on her way to the place of execution. It is to take place in public. We've tried to persuade her not to go, but she says she wants to see it all."

"Does she really want to?" I asked.

"Yes, she wants to be with him when it happens. There's nothing to be done, she's like that."

I walked in a wide circle around the group, but I still could not see the woman's face. Then I whispered her name. She heard me and turned her face toward me and looked at me. For a little while she looked at me!

One morning the police car from the mainland drove up. Two constables got out and introduced themselves politely. Handing me a letter in a greasy brown envelope, they said it was addressed to me from Johan Andersson at Skir. He had hanged himself, presumably several days ago. The doctor couldn't say for sure until after the post-mortem.

Anna was standing in the doorway, holding one hand to her mouth as though to check a cry. One of the constables asked if I would mind reading the letter so that they could then make use of it during the investigation: they couldn't exclude the possibility of murder. Johan had a severe bruise over one eye and distinct marks of blows and kicks on his body.

Dear Andreas!

An hour or two ago some people were here and said I was a villain and that now I was going to be punished for it. I said I was innocent, but they wouldn't listen. They took me by the hair and dragged me out into the yard. There they began to strike my head with their fists and to spit on me. I saw who they were all right but I don't intend to give them away, for what good can come of my mentioning them by name. One of them, it was one of the younger ones, picked up a big stone and struck me on the head with it. I got confused and said I was innocent. They said that if I confessed they would leave me alone and not strike me any more. Then I said I would confess and then they stopped hitting me in the face with their fists. They stood me up against the wall and told me to talk. I said anything that I thought they might like to hear. When I couldn't think of any more they knocked me down. One of them stood over me and pissed in my face but I couldn't shield myself as I was very tired. I cannot understand what came over them, they were like madmen although they had promised not to hit me any more if I confessed. They started kicking me as I lay there. My spectacles were trodden on and broken and my false teeth fell out of my mouth and later I couldn't find them. At last I don't know what they did to me, as I fainted. When I came to they had disappeared with their cars and I could go inside. I felt now that I didn't want to go on living, as I could no longer look anyone in the face.

So I don't want to live any longer. I am writing this letter to you, dear Andreas, because you have always been good to me and have always asked after my health. With best wishes. Johan Andersson.

I gave the letter to the police. We talked for a few minutes about this and that in connection with Johan, then they saluted and went off in their car. I looked around for Anna. She was no longer there.

I looked for her in the other room. She was not there either. I went up to the loft. There I saw her in a far corner. She was kneeling with hands clasped. I asked her what she was doing.

"I am praying for Johan," she replied without looking up.

I told her to stop that damn silly acting. Anna asked me to leave her alone. I lost my temper still more and sat down on the stairs.

"You're only praying for your own sake."

"Go away," Anna shouted, "go away and leave me in peace!"

"Awful acting," I said and went slowly down to the kitchen.

I rode to Skir on my bicycle. They had not yet taken the dead man away; they went around making notes and photographing. I asked if I could go in. Yes, I could. Johan was lying on his dirty bed in the room inside the kitchen. He looked horrible, but his hands were not injured. I couldn't help touching his right hand: lean, dirty, chapped with heavy work, black nails sticking out, and raised, vulnerable, twisting veins. It was almost unbearable. Two women came in. They were his sisters, and whispered together. One of them pulled open a drawer and said there was only a lot of rubbish, there was nothing worth taking. They went out again, giving me a curt nod. Johan and I were left alone. It was quite silent. A hard sunbeam moved on the dark, grubby wallpaper behind the dead man's head.

(Anna)

God, formerly I lived near You. I put out my hand in the dark and touched You! You punished me and knew why. You enclosed me in Your forgiveness and I rested. Away from You I am worried, always hunted, never safe. I try to do right but do wrong. I want to be truthful but live in a lie. I make an effort to think clearly but move about in a confusing gloom.

God have mercy on us all. Do not turn away from our cry. If You are ashamed of Your creation and want to obliterate it, then do not destroy us in this slow way. Hurl Earth from its orbit and let it fall into the void beyond Your knowledge. Put out our light, silence our screams, and let us be annihilated in a moment.

God, free me from myself, free me from my prison, free me from life's fever.

PART FOUR

I sat at my work, writing out a fair copy. I had a headache, presumably from some infection. Anna was sitting in the kitchen busy with her translation. Her typewriter announced great diligence.

"Am I disturbing you with this typing?"

"No, my dear, it's all right, this work I'm doing now is purely automatic."

"Are you sure it doesn't disturb you, it makes a frightful clatter, this old machine. I've nearly finished, then I'll write it out by hand and that can't disturb you."

"You're not disturbing me in the least."

"How do you feel?"

"I've a headache. I suppose it's the weather or else I'm in for a cold."

"Poor Andreas, shall I get you something hot?"

"Yes, please."

"I'll just finish this chapter. It's really quite exciting."

Then silence. My aching eyes closed, my fingertips against the eyelids, and I dreamed, more or less like this:

A white body with broad hips and big breasts. She had thick red hair, a bored laugh, and calm, dark eyes. Suddenly she moved inside my eyes: Katarina. She sat on my chest, pressing against me, she slid down and her nails scratched my skin. She laughed and raised her arm in a slow arching movement. She floated to and fro above my eyes, forcing her way deeper and deeper into my soft fever. Her foot was small and hard, with a high instep and red toenails. Red toenails are ugly—they look like a disease. The sudden pain of her sharp teeth. "Be quiet, Andreas, you have the wrong voice. Grip me tight around the hips. It feels nice."

She lay on the bed with knees drawn up and hands against the insides of her thighs. She breathed so violently that I thought she was sick. I was free at last, liberated but soon prisoner in a new obsession. She always came back, the smell of her hair surrounded us. I remember shouting at her to come back. She would come back, she pulled on one stocking, a hairpin fell to the floor, yes she would come back, but now it was difficult. I stretched out my hand and held it between her thighs, which were still moist. She sank down toward the bed. "I'll come back, do you hear what I say?" She embraced me, the black eyelashes quivering above the wide-open darkness of the eye. The broad, damp hand sought my hand. "I will come back." She used to undress over by the window, quietly, dispassionately, almost matter-of-factly.

"I think I'm pregnant, you see, it's all to hell, I don't want a child, not by you at any rate. How do you like my new bra? It's a bit tight actually, my breasts have swollen the last few days. Can't you see they're much bigger? And I'm ten days past my time. I thought I was hard to make pregnant, but it just goes to show."

She tiptoed on bare feet up to the bed. She turned her dark, calm, rather veiled eyes toward me and I saw her mouth, the thick underlip and the softly turned-up corners.

"One gets quite the wrong idea about you, Andreas, that's what is so annoying. You look so real, so normal, so healthy and harmonious. It's quite ridiculous. And you behave in such a wise, judicious way. You do. But when I'm in bed with you, right down inside I feel your misery. Do you know what it is? You have cancer of the soul. You should have an operation, you should have radiotherapy and medicine. Not that there's much hope, you have tumors everywhere. You will die a horrible death, I think it will be suffocation. It can't be avoided, but perhaps it can be postponed."

Her breasts regarded me gravely. She combed her hair. She

looked at herself in the mirror, she put on lipstick, she scented herself, she gazed at her body. She took a step and everything was changed, the room, the light, the disgust. Katarina rose toward the ceiling, sun reflections from sparkling water struck against her skin. She floated, reeled, and was attenuated; the reflections cut her to pieces and the red hair waved like seaweed.

"What are you doing?" Anna asked.

"I'm sitting and looking at a photograph."

"Hope it's not an old flame of yours."

"No, what makes you think that," I replied.

"What are you thinking about?" Anna asked from her kitchen table and the work she was making such strides with.

"I'm thinking about cancer, and it frightens me," I replied truthfully as I pressed my fingertips to my eyelids. There was a strange silence in the other room. "What are *you* thinking about?" I asked, mostly out of politeness.

"I'm not thinking of anything, I'm thinking of the lies," Anna replied in a dry voice.

"What lies?" I asked. She didn't answer, merely sighed.

Getting up from the kitchen table, she tidied her papers, then opened the pantry door. She took out a rather large bowl full to the brim with milk. She wanted to pour out a glassful. I sat watching her clumsiness. She turned out toward the room, tried to push the pantry door shut with her elbow; the milk slopped over, and she gave me a desperate, appealing look but I pretended not to see. She took a limping step out onto the floor. The milk slopped again, more violently. She tried to counteract it by tilting the bowl forward. Another step, and a still bigger puddle on the floor. "*Andreas,*" she called in despair, dropping the bowl. It shattered on the floor and the milk splashed in all directions. She stretched out her hands, her face unbearably appealing. I took her in my arms.

Embracing each other like this had become our fragile protection against the outside world, against our own moments of disintegration and horror. Words gave no relief, they were long since damaged by misuse, but by pressing close against each other we could still save ourselves. It never took away the inner loneliness, but it soothed the frightened heart and for a few minutes broke the feeling of irrevocable disaster. It was long enough for us to be able to pluck up courage and forget what was actually happening around us. What was actually happening with us.

Anna surprised me with a violent outburst.

We had lived together for several months in comparative harmony. Occasionally there had been slight clashes which had resulted in quarrels and reconciliations. More often than not this bickering was due to a misunderstanding or a fit of bad temper—the words used were never venomous or infected.

I don't know where or how it started. Anna was more silent than usual and retired with her work immediately after breakfast. I went out into the yard and started chopping wood. The whole time I had a premonition, a heavy feeling of fear and uneasiness. I heard her approach but didn't turn around. I went on splitting the tough logs of pine. She stood silent for a moment.

"I only want to tell you I'm leaving tomorrow. I would have gone today, but I've too much packing to do."

I stared at her, uncomprehending. She took a few steps toward me and I saw that her leg was troubling her. Her face was bloodless; black shadows were drawn under her eyes, which were bright with hatred. I replied that I was naturally interested to hear what had caused her to make her decision.

"*You* ought to know that."

She was very close now, I felt her breath, it stank with hatred.

We stood for a long time abusing each other. I recall it almost like a picture drawn by some bystander: by the woodstack behind the outhouse stand two beings who are completely relegated to each other, miles away from other people; they revile each other; one of them is holding an axe, which he grows more and more conscious of; around these two is the spring day with birdsong, rippling water, and a bright light. She spoke with a strange, somewhat lighter voice, expressing herself in a kind of grotesque literary language which I had never heard her use before.

I waited to see what would happen. I knew the exact word, the weapon. It gave me a kind of gaiety, a secret advantage which she must have felt, as her rage increased. The word is: "The farewell letter. I know your lie. I have gone straight through you and you are worthless." I began to entice her, her lack of self-control seemed to get more and more interesting. I could feel my heart beating heavily and slowly, the blood moving sluggishly through my head and a purely physical sense of well-being spreading through my body. The feeling of something decided once and for all was like security all around me.

> *Suddenly I saw my left hand around her throat. The edge of the axe cut deep into her broad white forehead, shattering the nose; the eyes opened wide and burst. I heard the dull thud of my second blow and I saw the blood gush out of the thick hair and the flap of skin whiten around the axe-head. I felt her hands still scratching at my clothes. I saw the mouth open in a shriek, which was stifled by the blood pouring out. She tried to crawl away and I buried the axe between her shoulders and she sank down on her belly with one knee drawn right up to her chin.*

Throwing down the axe, I took a few paces back from her. She turned away, holding one hand to her eyes as if she were starting to cry. I asked as calmly as I could if we shouldn't try to talk to each other after all. She shook her head. The hatred drained away, the desire to say the killing word was no longer there. I saw our wretchedness and was ashamed. She went slowly into the house. I followed her. She stood in the kitchen drinking water. She was trembling with emotion.

Slowly we became ourselves again.

At night we couldn't sleep. We were still much too upset, but we did everything to get close to each other, to try to bridge the gulf that had opened between us.

"We ought to take a trip somewhere, Andreas! We ought to get away from here. Don't you think we could talk to someone and borrow a few thousand? I know it would mean so much to us both. What are you thinking about, Andreas?"

"When you speak of that trip I want so much to say yes. I want to say that I'll have a word with Elis, he can probably lend us some money. At the same time a wall grows up. I cannot speak. I cannot show you that I am glad. I see your face and know that it is you. But I can't reach you. Do you understand what I mean?"

"I understand what you mean. I understand very well."

"I am outside. I am the one who has shut myself out. Or who has fled, as someone put it. At last one is so far away that . . ."

"I know, Andreas. I know how strange it . . ."

"Yes, it is strange. I want to be warm and tender and alive and I want . . . I want to make a move. You know how it is, don't you?"

"Yes, I know. I understand. It's like in a dream. You want to move, you know what you have to do but the body won't obey, the legs won't function, the arms are as heavy as lead and you try to talk but can't."

"I am so frightened of being humiliated. It's an everlasting misery. I have allowed myself to be humiliated ever since I was a child. And I have accepted the humiliations and let them sink into me and there they have stayed. Do you know what I mean? Do you understand me?"

"Yes, I know what you mean, Andreas. I understand."

All this, our quiet reciprocity, all this shook me and I felt I would start to cry.

"It's terrible to be a failure. Everyone thinks they can give me good advice. Everyone thinks they have a right to tell me what to do. Their well-meaning contempt. And then the distance, the coolness. The short desire to tread softly on something alive. It's . . . I can't talk about it."

"I understand what you mean. You needn't . . ."

"I am dead, Anna. No, I'm not dead, that's wrong and melodramatic. I'm not dead at all, but I live without self-respect. I know it sounds absurd and pretentious, since nearly everybody has to live without a sense of self-esteem, humiliated at heart, half stifled and spat upon. They're alive and that's all they know. They know of no alternative, and even if they did they would never reach out for it. Can one be sick with humiliation? Is it a disease that we have all caught, that we have to live with? We talk a lot about freedom, Anna. But isn't freedom a terrible poison for anyone who is humiliated? Or is the word freedom merely a drug which the humiliated use in order to be able to hold out. I can't live with all this, I have given up. Sometimes it's almost unbearable, the days drag by and I think I'll be suffocated by the food I swallow or the shit I get rid of or the words I say or the light, the daylight that comes every morning and shouts at me to get up, or the sleep which is always dreams that hunt me here or there, or merely the darkness that rustles with ghosts and memories. Do you understand how it is, Anna? I'm not asking for sympathy, it's not a question of sympathy. There's not the slightest reason to be sorry for me. I share my doom with millions and millions of people and I know that they are silent and humble. Usually I pretend that this is the way it is to be and I shut up. But it would be so wonderful if you could understand. Just for a moment. You save yourself by praying to God. No, I didn't mean to be nasty. Have you ever thought that the worse off people are, the less they complain? In the end they are quite silent, living creatures with nerves and hands and eyes. Vast armies of victims and hangmen and the light that rises and falls, heavily, and the cold that comes and the darkness and the heat and the smell. *But they are all quiet.* I am not afflicted, do you know what I mean? I have only been spat on and I sank into spittle. No, that's not true either. Forgive me, Anna. We can never leave here. Wherever we find ourselves, wherever we go, we are on this island. I don't believe in any move. Do you understand what I mean? Don't be angry with me, Anna. Please understand what I mean. My dear. Try to listen beyond the words. I am so grateful that you exist. It is like a moment's reprieve. Dear Anna. My dear. Don't be cross with me. My dear."

"I'm not cross. I understand. I'm not cross."

The fiery glow from Anna's dream was above the forest. We were suddenly aware of it. In the distance and then closer we heard the siren of the fire engine. A couple of miles away from us was a big farm, the biggest on the island: that is where the fire was. When we got there the fire had been more or less put out. The stable had burned down. In the twilight the butcher from the mainland stood leaning over the corpse of a horse. A small crowd had gathered. A stench of burned flesh and scorched skin hung over the yard. A little apart, Verner was standing, smoking. His pipe kept going out, he relit it with shaking hands. I went up to him. The butcher had rolled up his sleeves and was cutting into the dead, partly charred animal.

"Don't you know what has happened? I'll tell you. Someone made his way into the stable. He had a can of gasoline with him. He poured five gallons of gasoline over the horse, which was tied up, then he tossed a lighted match into the stall. He ran out quick as hell and locked the door from the outside, taking the key with him to make sure. The wretched horse stormed about inside and people stood outside trying to chop open the door. At last they got it open and the horse charged out and ran around blazing. It just wouldn't die."

(Elis)

It is hypocrisy to cry over the world's folly. It is absurd to be appalled at human cruelty. It is a waste of feelings to clamor for justice or decency. The sufferings of my fellow creatures do not keep me awake at night. I am indifferent in my own eyes and other people's. I function.

As Anna and I drove home we were silent at first, then I heard myself talking. This curious phenomenon: it is as if I myself were no longer talking, it is as if someone were talking through my mouth. I myself was remote, mute long since. I heard myself saying to Anna that I wanted to be free, I wanted my solitude back. I couldn't go on living, feeling affection, suffering, longing. Perhaps it would have been possible if I had loved her. And perhaps I did love her at first. I didn't know. Perhaps I had never loved. I wanted my silence back. Perhaps we could have succeeded, if we had loved each other. But we didn't. And that made it easier to part. More truthful, too. One must live in truth, at any rate according to Anna's way of looking at things. So now at last we were to be truthful. Anna didn't answer. She drove through the rain on the narrow, bumpy forest road. I could not see her eyes, only her profile. I was seized by a sudden rage at her silence and started to speak of Andreas' farewell letter: "Do you remember leaving your handbag behind one of the first times we met? You asked to use the telephone, do you remember?" Anna didn't answer. "Yes, you forgot your handbag and I found your husband's farewell letter in it and I read it. You've no success with your men, Anna. Either there's something wrong with you or else there's something wrong with your men. You who always talk of truth and of how one should live in truth. What a ghastly deception. I remember when you spoke of your marriage. All happiness. All love. Lies. Lies. It was all lies, Anna!"

Then I noticed that the car was going faster. In one swift instant

I understood what was happening. I asked her to stop, so that we could get out, so that we could calm down. I remember that I turned around, that the car was on fire. That I saw Anna's face in the flames, that I saw her eyes.

I remember running along the road. Then I felt the pain in my hands and face. An excruciating pain. I remember finding myself outside Elis's house. Eva came toward me. I remember calling to her, but I had no voice left, it was hardly more than a whisper: "Forgive me, forgive me, forgive me, forgive me, forgive me, forgive me, forgive me."

I remember her leaning over me.